MANAGING

by

LAUREL ASPEN

CHIMERA

Managing Mrs Burton first published in 2001 by
Chimera Publishing Ltd
PO Box 152
Waterlooville
Hants
PO8 9FS

Printed and bound in Great Britain by
Omnia Books Ltd, Glasgow

MANAGING MRS BURTON

Laurel Aspen

This novel is fiction – in real life practice safe sex

A – for experiment and encouragement.

Managing Mrs Burton

Paul Barlett stopped typing for a moment, stretched his cramped muscles and walked over to the French windows. Outside a perfect spring day enhanced the well-kept garden, which he admired perfunctorily before glancing at his watch.

No time for an easy stroll round the grounds just now, his five o'clock appointment was due in only another ten minutes. Just long enough to complete another couple of paragraphs.

No sooner had he resumed work at the PC than the concentration-enhancing silence was broken by the sound of his doorbell. Again Paul stopped work, but instead of irritation at this interruption of his endeavours he felt elated.

An early bird, mused Paul, leaving his favourite chair in the book-lined study to walk across the tiled lobby. Opening the front door he was momentarily confused at the sight of an elegant woman – his eyes made a covert visual assessment – in her mid-thirties standing on the doorstep.

'Mrs Burton?' Paul asked politely, the tone of his voice echoing his doubt.

'Yes, that's right,' she responded. 'You look confused; had you expected someone else?'

'I'm sorry… how rude of me, do come in,' Paul rapidly recovered his composure and waved his visitor across the threshold of the pleasant Edwardian redbrick with a welcoming smile. 'Sincere apologies, but the people your company usually send here are, er… rather different,' he added by way of partial explanation. 'Please do go on through to the study, on the right.'

As she did so Paul continued his earlier unspoken appraisal: a delicately-boned, attractive face, around five foot six inches tall, fashionably cut shoulder-length auburn hair, dark, well-tailored suit, stylish rather than trendy, high-heeled court shoes; all pretty much par for the middle-management course; businesslike enough to keep the female clients happy, sufficiently feminine to appease the worries of competitive male colleagues. And she wore it all well too – good posture and confident bearing.

Yet again he found himself puzzled. Surely the company had specified junior female ranks only in the contract? Still, no matter, he'd still a perfectly agreeable task to perform.

Once in the study he directed his guest to an upright chair by the window then resumed his former position at the desk, swivelling round in his upholstered seat in order to face her. Mrs Burton sat straight, sedate and clearly self-possessed, in marked contrast to the nervous, round-shouldered squirming displayed by previous occupants of that particular pew.

Reprising his earlier smile of greeting Paul commenced a by now familiar rhetoric.

'You have a letter for me I believe, Mrs Burton?'

'Yes, of course,' she replied, reaching into her bag to locate a sealed envelope marked *confidential*, which she handed to him.

'Hmmm, thank you.' Opening the correspondence with measured deliberation Paul drew out a neatly typed page of A4 paper headed with the Mitsuno International Corporation logo. Below were concise details of the bearer: *Mrs Sonia Burton, forty-one, Deputy Human Resources Director*.

Oh for the days when a personnel department was just that and no more, he thought fleetingly, but goodness, so much for his waning powers of perception – Mrs Burton was a full year older than he was but he'd defy anyone to guess as much. She'd certainly taken good care of herself. That trim figure must have taken some hard effort in the gym. Forcing his mind back to the letter Paul read on… ah, this was what he'd been seeking.

As part of the contractually binding procedure signed and agreed by the employee, Mrs Burton – having made serious errors of judgement and displayed a poor attitude to her superiors – is to receive medium grade corporal punishment from the Disciplinary Officer.

He looked up, deliberately making eye contact, which she returned without blinking.

'You know why you are here, I assume,' he said.

'Yes.'

'And you know what's going to happen?'

'I work in human resources, I know what the contract requires,' she replied, unflustered.

A brief tense pause followed. Paul had to admire her sang-froid; at this point they'd usually start making excuses or tearfully pleading for clemency.

Mrs Burton spoke again; the voice disrupting his reverie was tinged with amusement. 'I'm not what you envisioned am I?'

So unexpected and forthright was the query Paul found himself answering before he'd time to think. 'Indeed not,' he admitted frankly, 'most people Mitsuno send here tend to have the title Miss, or more likely, Ms. Usually junior admin grades and, I don't wish to offend, average age about twenty-one.'

'Which I'm far from being,' agreed Mrs Burton, evenly. 'But then you're not what I imagined either; how an earth do you come to be doing this?'

This time Paul was better prepared. 'I realise that you are accustomed to being in charge, asking forthright questions and expecting prompt answers.' He stood up, pausing to let her digest this concise evaluation. 'However,' he continued, in a firmer tone, 'on these premises that's my job.'

Mrs Burton glanced down at the polished floorboards for a moment, before responding. 'Fair enough, I consider myself charmingly rebuked, I'll try not to forget the proper purpose of this visit.' Her tone was ironic. 'But,' she added, looking up again, eyes twinkling, 'I'm still curious; professional habits die hard I'm afraid.'

Inwardly Paul struggled to suppress a grin. She was incorrigible. Usually he was lucky to get more than a few inarticulate mumblings from apprehensive filing clerks, red-faced and fidgeting, anxious to avoid eye contact; their fervent wish to get it over with and get the hell out. Mrs Burton was proving altogether quite different; sophisticated, intelligent, personable. Why, in different social circumstances the very sort of woman he'd…

Snapping out of what was in imminent danger of becoming an all too pleasant daydream Paul was careful to keep his expression neutral and voice measured. 'If you are skating on thin ice you may as well dance,' he sighed in resigned recognition of her persistence.

Mrs Burton's gaze followed him around the room; he preferred to walk as he spoke. She too was practised at making personal assessments: Paul Bartlett looked to be around five foot ten with the strong, slender build of a regular racquet sports player. Thankfully not some wimpish 'new man' – the very phrase made her shudder – but authoritative without being overbearing or a bully, educated but neither arrogant nor a swot.

Brown eyes – unusual in someone with blond hair – and of a similar age to herself. His clothes, like the slightly eclectic furnishings and décor of the room, demonstrated good taste. In her experienced judgement an altogether very pleasing package.

'Since you ask,' he continued, bringing her sharply back to the present, 'I was a hack on the street of shame, pretty damn successful too, but a change in personal circumstances – that's a polite way to describe a generous redundancy settlement and my wife running off with her boss – brought me here. New start, far from the maddening crowd, those sorts of clichés.

'I was doing quite nicely as a writer of erotic fiction, for those various paperback imprints that have become so popular in the last few years. Middle class pornography really; all text, no pictures, supposedly written for women but in reality usually bought by men.

'A couple of year ago Mitsuno decided to base its European HQ in the town, attracted by the success of the university and the fact London is only sixty miles away. You certainly don't need me to tell you they are by far the biggest employer and, when it comes to wages, most generous employer. Jobs with them are highly sought after and, it seems, people will do anything to keep them.

'A section of their massive publishing empire turned out to be the imprint I was writing for – apparently acquired as part of an earlier corporate takeover deal. I don't think Mitsuno even knew they owned it at first. Anyway, one day, completely out of the blue, no forewarning, nothing, two very serious Oriental men turned up on the threshold. They'd looked at my stuff, which tends to centre around a lot of mild S&M and CP scenarios, wondering if I knew anyone who could enforce their unique code of employment.

'It had worked wonders for productivity and company performance in Japan, they said, but since it was hitherto untried in Britain they felt it prudent to sub-contract out the "hands-on" end, if you'll pardon the pun. As a former professionally cynical hack I couldn't believe they were serious at first, but on hearing how much the firm was prepared to pay, I volunteered.

'So here I am, here you are, and that's quite enough chitchat. Stand up, please.'

Surprised by the sudden change of tone, just as Paul had intended she should be, Mrs Burton was on her feet before she realised it. He continued to walk slowly around the room.

'A medium disciplinary punishment,' he intoned solemnly, 'unusual for a first offence, incidentally, involves a spanking and a caning – in that order, understood?'

'Yes,' Mrs Burton's look was unwavering, her voice

steady, but something in the way she ran her tongue across her lips betrayed the nervousness she'd thus far done so well to conceal. Too late to stop now, she thought. A nervous thrill, part fear, part anticipation, coursed through every centimetre of her body.

'Usually, Mrs Burton,' he continued sternly, 'Mitsuno miscreants go across my knee for a hand spanking, but since it hardly seems right and proper to treat you in the same manner as a recalcitrant eighteen-year-old typist, we'll do things a little differently on this occasion.

'If you would please hand me your jacket and be so good as to place the chair you are sitting on in the exact centre of the room we can start proceedings.'

Undisputedly the master of ceremonies, Paul allowed a further hint of steel to creep into his pre-emptory commands. Mrs Burton obeyed without hesitation, surprised to find a strange sense of security in doing as she was bidden. With an unfamiliar, but not altogether unpleasant feeling of surrender, she slipped off the jacket and handed it to Paul before moving the solid hardwood furniture to the location directed.

'Thank you. Next, kneel on the seat please, face the back and raise your skirt to the waist.' Did he sound as matter-of-fact as he intended? In truth, watching this curvaceous mature woman do his bidding was infinitely more arousing than chivvying any number of skinny youngsters into position.

Mrs Burton knelt on the seat cushion as instructed. Someone else was calling the tune for a change; whatever happened next would be no responsibility of hers. With a mixture of relief and pride she carefully drew the hem of her just-above-knee-length skirt up to her waist, excited by the deliciously naughty sensation of revealing herself to a complete stranger – and a good-looking stranger, at that.

Paul wasn't disappointed by the view; firm, flawless buttocks surmounted long shapely legs. What's more, she was wearing stockings.

'Right, hands gripping the back of the chair, please, and get ready.' He stood parallel to her hips and noted with pleasure how easy it was to circle his left arm firmly around her waist, savouring an expensive perfume as he did do. With his right hand he tugged a pair of silky French knickers higher up onto her magnificent haunches; wider and more rounded than those usually presented to him, but by far the most tempting target he'd seen in along while.

Mrs Burton turned to look at her putative tormentor, her attractive face showing outward emotion to reflect the inner turmoil that now assailed her. 'Is this it?' she asked, struggling to stop her voice from trembling.

By way of reply Paul began to smack the scantily protected cheeks, following his customary, tried and tested method of alternating from one to another, warming up slowly. At first Mrs Burton rigidly maintained her prescribed stance as his palm cracked repeatedly down across the delicate material. After a while he stopped to observe her looking fixedly ahead, as if in a trance, lips pursed, hands tightly grasping the back of the chair.

By the time Paul halted for the second time Mrs Burton was becoming agitated. Her body jerked and twisted against his firm hold as her breathing audibly quickened. Paul resumed the spanking, watching her nether cheeks pinken, feeling her futile gyrations become evermore animated. Little gasps, punctuated by shrill cries of 'oww' and 'ahhh' left him in no doubt that the punitive message was hitting home.

Mrs Burton relinquished her tight hold on the chair, fluttering her hands behind her in a hopeless attempt to ward off further chastisement. Twice Paul found himself forced to grab her wrists, pinning them out of the way into the small of her back, and finally he gave vent to a mounting exasperation.

'Really, Mrs Burton, I'm shocked at you, behaving like a silly teenager. You simply must keep still, I've hardly started yet.'

'I'm sorry, you're right of course,' she said meekly. 'I used to be able to take a routine smacking such as this with ease, but I'm afraid I've become rather out of practice.'

'You've been spanked before?' Paul was taken aback. 'Most of the girls I deal with have never been dealt so much as a perfunctory slap, at home or school.'

'At boarding-school in the early seventies we were still caned across our knickers,' she told him. 'It only happened to me once; I got six for smoking and haven't touched a cigarette since, so it was obviously an effective deterrent, however much well-intentioned liberals would have as think otherwise.'

'And the spanking?' he pressed on, intrigued.

'My husband used to like to take me across his knee for an occasional bottom warming, but as foreplay, not punishment.'

'You didn't… I mean, it doesn't,' the mental images conjured by Mrs Burton's candid revelations had Paul

14

temporarily flustered. He took a deep breath and tried once more. 'It doesn't seem to fit the image of the modern independent woman.'

'I've had that argument with feminists before,' replied Mrs Burton wearily, 'and the answer is that I prefer to keep politics out of the bedroom. The whole point of feminism as I understand and support it is to be able to make our own informed choices. What are fantasies for if not to be lived out?

'Besides,' she went on, 'had they tried it before rushing to condemn, these contemporary puritans might have discovered that a hot sensual smart to a girl's rear end certainly livens up hum-drum married sex. Sadly that all stopped when the sod left me for his much younger secretary three years ago, and with an eighteen-year-old just starting university you can see why I'll do anything to avoid losing my job.'

'Anything except keep still and take your medicine,' observed Paul with characteristic good humour.

'You could go a little easier,' suggested Mrs Burton, archly.

'If you think you can talk me into letting you off lightly you can forget it. Someone in a senior position deserves a far sounder hiding than some foolish little low paid trainee, and that's just what you're going to get. I don't intend wrestling with you for the rest of the afternoon, but I will most definitely be finishing the job Mitsuno are paying me to do.'

With that assertion made plain Paul strode across the room and collected a second identical chair, which he placed back to back with the first. 'Bend right over, like this,' he said, grasping her wrists and putting them on

15

the seat. 'Hands supporting the weight of your upper body so you can't move to protect your bottom.'

He spent another couple of minutes positioning Mrs Burton to his satisfaction, silently enthralled by her aura of simmering sensuality. 'Knees slightly apart for balance, skirt right up out the way, knickers down to your knees.' He'd remember the erotically tactile sensation of sliding the shiny material of her knickers over her hips and down her thighs for weeks to come.

'That's better,' he added, finally content with arrangements. 'Now, since I'm wearing out my palm to no avail we'll complete the spanking with this.' As he spoke he crossed to a small cupboard in the corner of the study and produced an old-fashioned wooden-backed hairbrush. Mrs Burton, glancing in his direction, caught a glimpse and groaned a quiet protest.

'Oh no, please, that'll hurt dreadfully. Put me over your knee instead; I'd rather humiliation than suffering.'

Paul gently tilted her chin to look directly at him.

'In that cupboard I've a collection of tawses, paddles, and straps which can do a lot more damage than a simple Mason Pearson, so you'd be well advised not to complain and keep your delinquent backside still.'

Placing a steadying hand on the small of her back, he resumed his far from onerous task, methodically whacking every centimetre of the exposed flesh with the oft-used wooden wonder until the surface turned from pink to crimson.

Mrs Burton reacted with a series of yelps, squeals, and a lot of undignified wriggling. Her face blushed red as her posterior danced under a steady stream of blows. Satisfied that the upper reaches of her trembling orbs were now glowing nicely, Paul transferred his rhythmic attentions to the crease where buttock and thigh meet.

'Oh no, no, no,' she shrieked. 'Yeow! No... oh *please* stop. Oh my poor bum!' Mrs Burton's self-possession and poise were rapidly deserting her, and as the facade of control slipped even further she gave voice to a stream of decidedly unladylike epithets.

Ignoring her squeals of protest Paul continued with the thorough tanning of her behind, causing the lushly rounded flesh to bounce and judder at each further searing impact. Legs kicking wildly, her thighs involuntarily parting to show the deep shadowy crease between her burning buttocks, labia gleaming moistly through the tight fair curls. No longer in control, Mrs Burton's sole concern became concentrated on halting the searing pain that scorched every inch of her hurt-filled hindquarters.

'Almost finished,' announced Paul, running his hands across the glowing cheeks that radiated heat to the touch, fondling each buttock in turn, soothing and stroking, affording his victim an all too brief respite. 'I want you to count the final dozen out loud, please,' he said.

Humiliation complete, Mrs Burton struggled to find her voice.

Whack! 'One, thank you, sir,' she began without prompting.

Crack! 'Owww... two, thank you, sir.'

Slap! 'Three, ow, ow, ow, thank you, sir...'

With three final humdingers Paul reluctantly deemed stage one of the medium disciplinary punishment complete. 'Get up, please, leave your skirt and knickers exactly as they are and go and face the wall with your hands on your head. No rubbing,' he instructed.

Slowly and stiffly Mrs Burton complied, soundly spanked and perfectly obedient, lips wet and eyes brimming with incipient tears. As she stood, squirming from one foot to another, her bum-cheeks clenching of their own accord, Mrs Burton was only too aware of the sorry spectacle she was presenting to Paul's unabashed view; knickers around her knees, a bum that seemed to have grown in size blazing like a beacon. So much for her carefully cultivated executive image. What had she got herself into?

Paul spent another couple of congenial minutes observing her deliciously dishabille discomfort before relenting. 'All right, now you can rub,' he said, a note of kindness in his voice.

Immediately her hands flew back to massage the hot, sore flesh, looking sadly over her shoulder at the ruby-red display. 'Thank goodness I didn't wear tights,' she observed ruefully. 'I'd never have been able to pull then back up over my poor tender bot.'

'Your poor tender bot's not finished with yet,' Paul reminded her, 'you've still six strokes of the cane to come before we're through.'

Mrs Burton looked dismayed, then with a heroic act of composure, breathed deeply and steeled herself for the inevitable denouement. 'There's no point in pleading for leniency, I suppose,' she observed sorrowfully, 'and since canings are traditionally given on the bare, these better come off.'

Down slid the panties, causing the lump in the front of Paul's fortunately loose-fitting chinos to become a tent pole.

'Blouse as well,' he heard himself say, exceeding the

Mitsuno disciplinary procedures by a mile and throwing caution to the winds. He stepped forward, carefully unbuttoned the white lawn cotton garment and helped it glide from her shoulders. Mrs Burton stood, gorgeous and unresisting – lower torso nearly naked in stockings, shoes and a suspender belt – the V at the top of her legs as noticeably damp as her eyes.

'In which case,' she added in a voice almost returned to its former strength, but an octave lower, 'there's precious little point in retaining this either.' Unfastening her bra she cast it aside to join the other items, freeing two full, erect-nippled breasts in doing so.

Paul, standing behind her, gently cupped one in each palm, relishing their weight and warmth. Words were rapidly becoming redundant. An electric tension, a shared appreciation of the moment linked them like telepathy.

'Where do you want me?' she inquired huskily, and Paul became aware that once more the estimable Mrs Burton was in danger of subverting his power, resuming command of the situation and leading events from what was supposed to be the penitent's position.

'Over the back of that,' he instructed gruffly, pointing to a large well-upholstered armchair. 'Grip the front legs, feet well apart, bottom right out. No need to count, just concentrate on keeping still. This is going to hurt, and I warn you, move and I'll have no compunction about repeating the stroke.'

His authority regained, Paul chose a thin malacca cane from the cupboard and took up position behind and to the right of the jack-knifed Mrs Burton, now bent fully over the chair back as directed.

She waited, well-toned body taut with apprehension,

sheer stocking-clad legs spread wide. Her constantly throbbing sore bottom thrust out prominently once again, revealing the most intimate details of hitherto hidden charms; head down, breasts unfettered, a near perfect submissive pose. Trembling, she awaited his will, unsure how and when this ritual would reach its conclusion.

Cruelly Paul flicked the cane through the air, watching the woman flinch at the sound of his experimental strokes. Then, mustering as much detachment as possible he slowly, systematically, laid on five parallel stripes, striking hard into the already ravaged flesh, letting each lingering hurt sink in fully before delivering its successor.

Every cut produced a shriek, frantic immodest weaving of hips and drumming of toes, but Mrs Burton now completely mastered, somehow managed to maintain her stance, retaining some small shred of decorum as her curvaceous hindquarters were soundly whipped. The final, diagonal 'gating' stroke caused loud cries of distress and floods of tears as it slashed a blazing trail across each of the previous marks, decorating her comely posterior like the coda to an agonising symphony.

'Well done, Sonia,' said Paul, with perfect sincerity, using her christian name for the first time. 'You took that caning extremely well, bravely and with fortitude. Now stay exactly where you are and I'll reward your perseverance with some cold cream.'

'Thank you,' replied Mrs Burton hoarsely, raising her tearful face to attempt a smile, 'that would be lovely.' Her scalding cheeks were a concentrated focus of physical suffering and discomfort, yet she felt strangely relaxed, purified and above all, aroused.

Searching the bathroom for some suitably soothing

ointment Paul prudently pocketed a packet of condoms. If his reading of the runes was correct, Mrs Burton, a tingling warmth steadily spreading through her loins, was ready for a rather different kind of rod.

Back in the study she remained in position, moaning softly as he massaged the cooling balm into her expertly beaten buttocks. Wordlessly she pushed back her hips, opening her thighs to accommodate him. Donning a condom and firmly holding Mrs Burton's slender waist, he slid easily into her generously lubricated sex, and soon moans of pain subtly changed in timbre as he screwed her inexorably to orgasm.

Two days later Mr Kenyati, European president of Mitsuno International, applauded politely as the meeting ended. 'A superb presentation, Mrs Burton, surpassing even your consistently high standards.' His deputy director, soon to be, if she did but know it, director of human resources, smiled back in acknowledgement, before walking gingerly from the conference room.

Strange, Mr Kenyati thought to himself, she moved like a recently thrashed trainee, but that couldn't be the case; senior managers were not, and never had been, subject to such strictures, and the thought was already fading as he turned to check the latest revenue figures.

A month later, bottom shifting restlessly on the seat of her company car, the newly promoted Mrs Burton takes a familiar detour, turning into an agreeably tree-lined road towards a detached Edwardian house. A tall fair-haired man stands waiting at the window. She is smiling. It is five to five on a summer afternoon…

Further Education

Ben looked around the room – a full house tonight. He enjoyed – or should that be appreciated? – the weekly evening class. Adjectives, adjectives everywhere but never the right one. Okay, *Contemporary Literature and Society* was a pretentious title but the tutor, a 'serious' novelist, had a light touch and an amusing style of presentation.

His fellow students were the usual mixed bunch; would-be writers in the main, anxiously analysing the work of already published authors, concentrating assiduously, taking things very seriously.

Others were more laid back, simply glad of a break from the kids or a chance to make new friends. They'd nothing to prove; future Booker prize juries could relax.

And which category, mused Ben, do I fall in? Piles of books around his flat revealed a genuine interest in the subject, but if he were honest – one of his better traits – he wouldn't be averse to a brief encounter either.

For some reason the only other two males in the class had dropped out in the early stages leaving Ben the sole remaining representative of his gender. Anxious not to dominate conversation, he'd opted for a low profile. I'm a new-ish man after all, he'd reasoned.

A couple of female students flashed smiles. Social interaction had progressed to the friendly chat in the canteen stage; polite opinions swapped, jokes benignly smiled at. Could this week's subject: *Sex in Modern Writing – Erotica or Pornography*? possibly be why so many souls had turned out on a wet April night? True, romantic fiction had also got a good crowd, but he'd a feeling his cynicism was well founded.

'Hi Ben,' a warm familiar voice jolted him from his reverie and a smiling young woman drew up an adjacent chair. Ben beamed back a greeting, but had no time to talk before the lecture began.

As the tutor launched into a brief preamble, read a couple of college notices, distributed a booklist, Ben stole a series of furtive glances at his immediate companion; just to practice the character sketch techniques they'd learned last term.

Nicola was her name. Quiet, but certainly not shy. Friendly, if a little guarded. A responder rather than an initiator. Green eyes, red hair, mid-twenties, around five foot four with a slim, shapely figure. Face it, he fancied her.

Her voice jolted the daydream-believer back to reality. 'It's warm in here,' she whispered, shrugging off her blouson jacket. The jumper beneath emphasised a slender waist and small, firm breasts.

Flicking back her shoulder-length curls, suddenly aware of Ben's gaze, she smiled affectionately then rummaged in her bag for a pair of round, steel-framed spectacles: 'I'd better put these on; don't want to miss anything.' Ben was still absorbing the implications of that remark when the tutor introduced the guest speaker.

Louise Lasalle was in her early forties, extremely good-looking, confident and clearly well educated. Resembling a successful businesswomen rather than any stereotype of a writer, she was elegantly and expensively dressed.

She began her discourse with some historical examples of erotic writing – Chaucer, Shakespeare, the Decameron, before moving on to practical tips: how to handle commissioning editors, which of the various permutations of acceptable subject matter an aspirant author might consider. The first half of the session passed both quickly and divertingly, ending with a promise from Louise to throw the forum open for questions and discussion after the break.

'There's nothing new under the sun,' said Ben to Nicola as he fetched her a coffee. Without intending to he'd reached the canteen first where, to his surprise and pleasure, she'd made a beeline across the room to join him.

'They certainly weren't short of inhibitions in the past,' she agreed, 'but it's the second half, the more contemporary stuff, I'm looking forward to. I think we'll find things get a bit more controversial.'

Her guess proved correct. Louise was explaining the increase in erotic stories for women when the argument started. With a mixture of cowardice and prudence Ben, as token male, kept his head down and his own counsel while barbed words flew about his ears.

An especially tetchy teacher named Angela Dwight took the line that such paperbacks were just another way for men to make money from women.

'As a writer and a women,' Louise pointed out gently, 'I feel far from exploited—'

'We shouldn't be allowing them on the bookshelves,' cut in Angela, who despite her education clearly hadn't absorbed the difference between aggression and assertion. 'Erotica, pornography, it makes no difference; people must be protected.'

'And look what strange bedfellows you end up with,' replied Louise sagely. 'Religious fanatics, right-wing bigots; people that love to proscribe. You say you're a feminist Angela,' she continued, 'but did it ever occur to you that the self-appointed moralists you seem so anxious to court are the same people that want to deny women any choices at all?'

'That's true,' said a nearby voice, and Ben turned around to see Nicola on her feet. 'I've bought and enjoyed some of these books, I don't need your protection.'

'Like Louise's spanking stories I suppose,' sneered Angela sarcastically. 'Women being beaten or bound; what a wonderful use of our newfound freedom of expression.' Nicola reddened but stood her ground, however it was Louise, still calm and authoritative, who answered.

'You're twisting the argument again, Angela, You just can't seem to appreciate the difference between fantasy and reality. A lot of my readers are every bit as professionally and personally powerful and successful as you. If they want to act out a submissive fantasy with a trusted partner it doesn't make then servile, subjugated or second-class. Simply it's a matter of being honest about one's sexuality. By writing our own erotica we make our own choices.'

The controversy was still raging when the session finally overran.

Ben was intrigued, and not just by the debate, although it had been instructive to see women arguing in favour of one of his favourite fantasies. He'd also gained an insight as to where Nicola was coming from, and it was somewhere he'd very much like to go. Now or never, he thought as they filed out of the building.

Nicola stood in the corridor, chatting to Louise. 'Fancy a drink?' he asked. He'd intended the question for her alone, but fifteen minutes later the three of them were ensconced in the saloon bar of the *Swan*.

'Did you enjoy reading my books?' Louise enquired innocently. Her enquiry had been directed at Nicola. 'Yes,' they both unintentionally answered at the same time, then laughed self-consciously at the revelation.

'Well, my stories do usually feature a good deal of CP—' Louise began.

'And sex,' Nicola interrupted.

'Of course,' Louise continued with a twinkle, 'but I'm interested in means as well as ends. Tell me,' she continued, 'is your interest in spanking purely literary, or have you ever indulged?'

The two younger people exchanged glances. 'No, not yet,' replied Nicola, 'but the idea sends shivers down my spine, and in the right situation with the right person, I believe would.'

Impressed by the courage of this intimate disclosure, Ben decided to follow suit. Somehow it felt easier to reveal such a long-held desire to a woman. 'I'd love to have a relationship in which I could be masterful – of course we'd be equal in ever other respect,' he added hastily, 'if I could just find a submissive partner.'

'If you'll forgive me flaunting my age and experience, I suggest you've found each other,' replied Louise. Ben suddenly became aware that Nicola was now sitting very close to him, and unprompted she reached for his hand.

'Let's not prevaricate,' continued Louise, smiling at this overt conformation of her intuition. 'You must both come to dinner this Saturday; perhaps we can provide food for thought as well. A personal tutorial for two special students.'

'A master class,' responded Ben with a grin.

'Exactly,' confirmed Louise. 'And between then and now I suggest you both read some of my stories, absorb the mood, study the characters and dress for the occasion. Oh, and you might like to bring some decent wine. Italian white would be good.'

'We'll be there,' said Nicola earnestly, and Ben realised that she'd made the decision for them both.

The dinner party was going marvellously. Ben felt relaxed and at ease. He'd an anxious moment earlier in the evening when Nicola had been nearly fifteen minutes late at the station, but finally she arrived, in no apparent rush and looking ravishing, to greet him with a far from sisterly kiss.

Louise and Phil, her partner, owned a large Victorian house in a pleasant north London suburb, decorated inside with taste, flair, and an eclectic selection of art.

Ben quickly observed a difference in Louise's demeanour, noticeably more subdued than at their previous meeting. Phil cooked while she welcomed and entertained, yet despite this apparent role reversal, within these walls a man was clearly in charge.

Just as Louise's appearance belied her occupation, so too did Phil's. Tall and solidly built, with a Yorkshire accent and that county's celebrated directness, he turned out to be an English professor at a nearby university.

Adept at getting his initially somewhat overawed guests to talk freely he proved an informed and witty host, able without apparent effort or command, to subtly direct the evening's events.

The meal concluded, Ben noticed Louise sitting silently, hands in her lap, eyes following the flow of conversation but making no comment. An electric tension began to suffuse the atmosphere of what might otherwise have been taken for an ordinary dinner party.

'Always an enjoyable part of the proceedings,' observed Phil, expansively. 'The anticipation of things to come. I gather Louise has promised you two novices some instruction in our ways.

'Well, Saturday evenings here are set aside for Louise to account and atone for her sins, and for me to dispense discipline as I see fit. If you, Nicola, and you, Ben, would care to join us we'd be delighted to share our knowledge and experience.'

'I'm willing,' replied Nicola decisively.

'Me too,' confirmed Ben, experiencing an agreeable thrill of adrenalin-fuelled expectation as he spoke the words.

'Splendid,' Phil smiled. 'Now, you'll no doubt have noticed Louise has been looking a tad apprehensive this last half hour or so; and well she might. Her conduct over the last week – I won't bore you with the details – has earned her a traditional three-part punishment, which I now intend to commence. If you two would be so good as to follow us through to the next room, we can begin.'

The lounge was large and warm, atmospherically lit with up lighters and furnished with comfortable antiques.

'Proper punishments begin with a spanking,' Phil

pronounced. 'Only a bloody barbarian goes straight for a rod or switch. Build up gradually and be surprised how far you can go.'

Ignoring a suitable looking upright wooden chair he sat instead on a well-padded sofa, and catching Ben's quizzical expression he explained. 'I know in the magazines the unfortunate damsel touches the floor with hands and toes, but if you're intending to keep her there for more than five minutes it's hellish hard on the back.'

Taking Louise by the hand he drew her to attention beside him. She wore an elegant wool suit, silk blouse and black high heels. 'Lift your skirt, woman,' he ordered. Louise glanced around, as if only now aware of the expectant looks on the faces of her invited audience. Nervously she ran her tongue across her red lips, before obeying. From just above the knee she gradually inched the material up bare legs, teasingly revealing taut thighs and buttocks until at last it bunched around her waist.

Unhurriedly Phil turned Louise in a circle, running his hands over her silky-smooth, lightly suntanned flanks. She wore a pair of black lace-edged knickers, barely containing a full, firm backside.

Every inch a sensual woman, thought Ben, feeling the front of his trousers tighten. Next to him Nicola put on her glasses, and on the sofa Louise now languished across Phil's lap.

Slap, *slap*, *slap*… Phil applied his right hand to the rounded, pale cheeks. Elbows resting on the sofa cushions, chin in her cupped hands, Louise stared into the middle-distance as if entranced.

Some fifty or more smacks later Phil halted, and instead tugged her knickers tightly into the furrow that separated the two reddening globes. Louise jerked her hips agitatedly; the sudden switch from pain to pleasure occasioning her first audible response. Sighing contentedly she turned to observe her partner's ministrations.

'Quite sufficient a gradual warm-up,' said Phil, by way of reply. 'High time you had a proper spanking.'

Slap, slap, slap…

Nicola sat on the upright chair, leaning forward to gazed with rapt concentration as this live CP scenario unfolded. Ben noticed her wince in sympathy as noticeably harder smacks echoed like pistol shots around the room. Her skirt had ridden up revealingly, and he watched in fascination as she unconsciously clenched and unclenched her thighs.

The effect on Louise was clearly less erotic. Little yelps and moans now escaped her lips as she tried vainly to twist her body from Phil's tight, waist-encircling grip.

Another pause, Louise groaning in pleasure as Phil's hand again soothed the hot mounds and his finger explored hidden depths. Told to raise her hips she instantly obeyed, allowing Phil to slip the black panties to her knees.

Smack, smack, smack… Phil redoubled his efforts. Protesting loudly now Louise wriggled fiercely on his lap, earning a dozen scalding slaps to her thighs for her trouble. 'Women who struggle must pay the price,' announced Phil steadfastly. Ben stole another glance at Nicola, who remained fixated by the sight before her, one hand twirling her red hair.

Phil's hand descended six more times to conclude the first stage of his wife's ordeal. Tugged to her feet she stood, hair awry and dishevelled, in marked contrast to the manicured, self-possessed women of some minutes previously. Instinctively her hands flew to rub her burning bottom, now a uniform ruby-red.

'Oh no you don't.' Phil's directive was punctuated with a sharp slap to the front of each thigh, drawing a wail of complaint. 'Hands on head and into the corner, now!'

Fettered by her tangled knickers, Louise hobbled across the room to stand facing the wall, her dark glistening thatch just visible to three pairs of admiring eyes.

'Your turn I think, Ben,' said Phil mildly. 'I'm sure you can find an excuse to punish that pretty young person next to you.'

Ben was equal to the moment. 'I'm not sure I need one,' he replied in an assured voice. 'There again,' he added, after a piquant pause, 'I certainly do not like to be kept waiting by a date.'

Nicola's reaction to this new authoritative tone was not quite as he'd imagined. He'd expected to be treated to an expression of fey shock; contrarily she merely poked out her tongue. With one stride Ben covered the distance between them. Grasping her wrists he pulled the miscreant to her feet and, before she knew it, seated himself on the chair and pushed her over his lap. Drawing up her short pleated skirt with his right hand he reached with the left to deftly remove her glasses.

'Bravo, old chap,' said Phil, taking them from Ben while the latter surveyed his prize. Ignoring Nicola's token protestations he allowed his hands to glide over a pair of damson coloured briefs. Similar coloured suspenders were fastened to tan stockings.

'Now hang on a min...' Nicola's last-ditch plea for

clemency died on her lips as Ben swung down his arm. Resisting the temptation to spank too hard too soon he followed Phil's example and built up the tempo slowly, working skilfully to both chastise and arouse. Painted fingernails scrabbled at the rug, painted toenails in high strappy sandals kicked in the air.

Ten minutes later, pants around her ankles and bare bottom an angry pink, Nicola stood next to Louise, sneaking a glance over her shoulder to watch the men sip their wine in companionable, contemplative silence.

Phil's plan for the next stage of this practical introduction to the not-so-gentle art of CP proved ingenious. Plump cushions were placed at the two ends of an oak dining table and the knickerless women bent over them to lie face to face, legs apart and each grasping the other's wrists.

Walking over to a cupboard in the corner Phil took out two tawses which, judging from their appearance, had given sterling service over many years. He handed the lighter of the two to Ben, with the words, 'I'll go first, then you follow suit.'

Taking his place, Ben watched carefully as Phil raised the burnished two-tailed leather strap to shoulder height before bringing it down across the crown of his wife's upturned hindquarters.

Louise cried out, sliding forward on the polished tabletop. The twin hillocks of her cheeks flattened with the impact before springing back to their former spherical shape. Ben followed suit, but was disappointed to deliver a rather feeble sounding swat. Phil's turn again, and a satisfying crack of leather on skin drew another shout from Louise who, were it not for Nicola's firm grasp, would no doubt have shot bolt upright.

Ben tried again, but still had not mastered the technique. Nicola's cry was one of genuine anguish and, as her feet performed an agonised tap-dance, he was horrified to see an angry red weal form on her right thigh. He swallowed the urge to apologise as Phil blithely advised, 'A little too far to the right. Don't let the tails curl round or you miss the proper target'.

Fortunately Ben hit his stride with stroke number three, going on to deliver five crisp, blazing stripes, one after another, each accompanied by increasing cries of woe.

'Very good,' observed Phil. 'You're quite getting into the swing of things.' He ran his hands reflectively across Louise's now blotchy, blazing buttocks. 'Another four should fit the bill nicely – tell you what, let's try to synchronise them.'

It was an image Ben hoped he'd never forget. A pair of tawses concurrently swishing down to punish two already very sore bottoms whose owners, self-possession rapidly deserting them, yelled and twisted in unison, tightly grasping each other's hands for support and succour. Taking his cue from Phil, Ben ensured his final cuts lashed low into that supremely sensitive area where buttocks and thighs merge, forcing the recipient up onto her toes. Louise's lip trembled, her faced flushed but, although breathing rapidly, she maintained her composure.

Less cushioned to resist the searing impacts by the tenth stroke Nicola's mascara was running in rivulets down each cheeks, her high heels drumming on the polished parquet. She looked absolutely gorgeous, thought Ben, at once proud, vulnerable and thoroughly dominated. His erection neared critical mass as he floated on the biggest high of his life.

'Feel free to rub,' said Phil expansively as, a thorough tawsing completed, the two women stood stiffly, tentatively reaching behind to gently knead their ravished nether regions.

'And finally,' he added, returning to the mysterious corner cupboard, 'the cane.' Again his choice of implement was rather heavier than Ben's. 'I suggest half a dozen for Nicky as it's her first time, but for Louise, who seems determined to be stubborn, the full dozen.

'Right woman, centre of the room,' he went on. 'You know the drill.'

Head held high, Louise did his bidding. Shedding her blouse and skirt en route she stood erect in just heels and bra, revealing that nature had allocated equally generous curves to the upper half of her body. Taking a deep breath she gracefully bent forward to grasp her ankles, feet half a metre apart.

Phil delivered half a dozen hard, unhurried strokes, spaced at roughly ten second intervals, leaving a legacy of neatly spaced parallel lines that would decorate her derriere for several days. Between each whack Louise struggled to maintain her stance but, despite the all too obvious pain searing through every nerve ending, failed to shed a tear.

'Very impressive, my dear,' said Phil affectionately, as she stood to once again rub the target area, 'but you're the architect of your own misfortune. Bend again please, knees together, legs straight, and this time push that bottom right out.

'The art,' he addressed this remark to no one in

particular, but spoke with the voice of one uttering a universal truth, 'is to know and respect your partner's limits, but each time take them just a fraction further. Louise has demonstrated self-control; I shall now exercise complete control.'

Ben and Nicola stared, speechless; this scenario was far beyond their dreams. Chastened and humiliated, Louise was nevertheless visibly very wet.

'Do you accept this final chastisement?' asked Phil quietly.

'I do, darling,' came the unhesitating reply.

This time the strokes fell rapidly, one after another, each criss-crossing those applied earlier. Squirming in pain Louise had tears in her eyes by the second, and to Ben's amazement was both smiling and sobbing by the sixth.

Having kept position throughout, Louise straightened as if released of a burden, to address the remaining participants. 'If you'll forgive us, we've some pressing business in the bedroom…' She paused, wincing as she massaged the corrugated globes. 'Please take your time to finish and make full use of the facilities.' Another pause, Phil strong and silent stood behind gently cupping her breasts in his large hands.

'I'm pleased to confirm you've both excelled at this first lesson,' he added with mock severity. 'Next month we're holding an advanced class. I look forward to your attendance.'

Their hosts departed, Nicola turned gingerly to Phil, wrapped her arms around his neck and kissed him long and hard, moulding her body to his as she did so.

'Just you wait your turn,' responded Ben firmly, as he

led her unprotesting to a well-upholstered arm of the sofa. Off came the pleated skirt, and the T-shirt followed. Two diminutive but prominent breasts, each nipple erect, were proffered. 'Not yet,' said Ben, his voice barely a whisper, but suddenly possessed by a confidence and authority he'd only previously imagined.

Having bent Nicola face down over the sofa's broad arm, legs straight and slightly apart, he stopped for a moment to survey his handiwork. Her glorious bottom positively radiated heat, angry red stripes embroidered the centre, and a livid crimson hue gradually faded as it spread to her flanks and thighs.

Ben left a long interval between each of the subsequent six strokes of the cane, allowing the full stinging effect to warm its way towards the glistening treasure awaiting him in the valley below. Her beautiful blush-red arse bore marks that would stay for several days, yet he'd not thrashed her hard. There had been no need.

'Now you've beaten me, what next?' she asked quietly, rhetorically, replacing the proffered spectacles, and a visible tremor of desire ran through her lithe body.

By way of reply he loosened his belt and grasped her hips. One step to heaven. Once more Nicola bent forward, then once again went up onto her toes, the heat from her beaten bottom firing her loins and suffusing his as her new lover thrust deep and hard inside her.

Three months later Nicola's first erotic novel was published to wide critical acclaim, even gaining plaudits from mainstream book reviewers. It was dedicated to: *My two oldest friends, Louise and Phil, and my new mentor, Ben.*

Motorway Madness

Hilly was furious; her daring surprise reduced to a humiliating farce, and all because that philandering bastard had been cheating on her.

An older wiser head might have blamed some of her predicament on boredom. Finals over, the judgement day of results still to come, Hilly occupied a desultory hinterland between university and the harsh realities of work. In no hurry to surrender her sybaritic lifestyle for the chaos of commuting and the tyranny of mortgage demands, she'd lounged around the town's cafés and parks enjoying the summer.

In a fake tapas bar Hilly had met Derek, several years older and allegedly 'something in the media'. A cosmopolitan line of chat and the vague promise of useful introductions drew her hook line and sinker into a brief affair. Someone less naïve would have spotted the pitfalls a mile away, but while Hilly's family were both rich and generous her experience of life was limited. Lacking the maturity and experience to tell such an obvious menopausal Lothario as Derek to get on his bike, Hilly realised too late she'd fallen for a sucker punch.

It had seemed such a good plan at the time. Derek was abroad on business for a few days, and restless and at a loose end, Hilly decided to honour his return with a special surprise. Until now they'd met only at her flat or on neutral ground – restaurants or hotels – but after their last liaison, as Derek snored away the effects of Hilly's youthful vigour and too much red wine, she'd done a little detective work and discovered his home address.

Carefully choosing something low-cut and flimsy, Hilly set off to make her dramatic entrance. Fortunately it was a hot day and the windows of Derek's suburban palace were open. As she skipped up the gravel drive, her mind full of amorous ploys, Hilly heard voices, one of them a woman's. Prudently she slowed her pace and listened, and a cold hand seemed to grab her heart.

For ten long dispiriting minutes Hilly crouched behind the shrubbery and experienced Derek's homecoming at second hand. It was all now so obvious. Derek was not only married but, judging from the sounds emanating from within, enthusiastically celebrating the fact.

Disappointment rapidly gave way to rage. In a blazing fury Hilly ran tearfully back to the road, leapt into her little convertible and screeched away down the street. With no clear idea where she was going she found herself on the motorway ring road. The wind in her hair and loud music on the stereo calmed her a little, and Hilly began to fancy herself in the role of a latter-day Thelma or Louise.

Speeding down the middle lane she was vaguely aware of the breeze blowing up her skirt, exposing not just tanned legs but the white triangle of her skimpy knickers. The temper-filled leap into her car had caused a couple of buttons on her blouse to come undone, revealing rather more than was decent of what, her male classmates had often commented although not in such decorous terms, was a generous bosom. What the hell, she giggled, overtaking a van and revelling in the lust-filled gaze of its occupants. They couldn't afford her, but she'd treat them to a flash all the same.

She drew level with the cab of a large articulated lorry, so close Hilly could feel the heat of the engine and smell the diesel fuel. What sort of tough guy controlled the tonnes of rolling metal, commanding and confident behind the wheel?

Whoever, she bet the poor sod would appreciate a glimpse of firm young flesh to liven up his life. Hilly tooted the horn, well aware that in looking down from his cab the driver would have a grandstand view of her assets. In reality, the man at the wheel looked neither poor nor old; young, fit and good-looking might have been a better description. Fortunately, of the two of them it was he who quickly returned his eyes to the road; revelling in her imagined allure Hilly was too busy practicing a provocative pout to notice the traffic slowing in front of them. There was no way she could stop in time to avoid the car in front. Desperately she wrenched the steering wheel, swerving in front of the heavy truck.

The squeal of brakes was ear splitting, burning rubber filled the air, and Hilly was convinced she would die. But no, somehow the truck missed her, swung onto the hard shoulder then, after a heart-stopping slalom, inched out back into the nearside lane.

Shocked and shaking uncontrollably Hilly drove on, her mind a maze of guilt and confusion. Luckily, after just a few miles she spotted a service area, drove in and parked the convertible in a remote spot. Gradually her breathing steadied and she stopped trembling. 'You fool, you bloody stupid fool,' she muttered self-pityingly, and reached to turn the ignition key for a miserable drive home.

Behind her came a hiss of air brakes. In the mirror she could see nothing but the front of an extremely large truck that, with a sinking feeling, she realised was the one she'd so nearly caused to crash. Her car was completely blocked in; there was no escape.

Without bothering to open the door a tall male form slung laconically into the passenger seat of the convertible. Frank blue eyes appraised her, and a calloused hand reached across and removed the ignition key. The silence hung oppressively, and scared witless, completely out of her depth, Hilly had no idea what to do.

'It wasn't just me you almost killed back there,' he said in a calm, well-spoken voice. 'That truck weighs thirty-eight tonnes, so just think of how many other people could have been wiped out if I'd lost control.' Ashamed and with no credible reply, Hilly turned away. Again he reached out, forcing her to face him. Incongruously she fixed her eyes on the tiger tattoo decorating his upper arm.

'I've come all the way from Marseille without mishap,' the driver continued grimly. 'Then less than ten miles from home I'm nearly wiped out by some spoilt brat,' he looked pointedly at her, 'who drives and flashes her tits at the same time. I ought to call the police.'

'No, please,' Hilly spoke for the first time, her voice tremulous. 'I know I don't deserve to be let off. I've been childish and stupid but if I went to court it'd mortify my parents.'

'So you do occasionally think of someone other than yourself?' He spoke sarcastically, but in softer tones.

40

'Where do you live?'

Hilly mumbled her address.

'Well, you're too shaken to drive home, that's for sure, but fortunately it's in the right direction so I can give you a lift. By the way, the name's Mike... and you are?'

'Hilly,' she said timidly.

'I can't say I'm in the least pleased to meet you, Hilly, but lock up your car and we'll get going.'

Mike helped her up into the cab. *Three Steps to Heaven*, said a wry caption painted just above the metal steps, and scrambling clumsily Hilly hauled herself inside. 'Amazing, there's so much room,' she gasped. 'You can stand up, and there's a bed!'

'Look closely and you'll find a fridge and a microwave, too,' replied Mike, climbing in behind her. 'Just as well, since this is home for two weeks at a time. Not quite enough room to swing a cat,' he continued, a hint of steel apparent in his voice, 'but ample space for your comeuppance.'

'What do you mean?' cried Hilly, suddenly afraid.

'You surely didn't expect to pull a stunt like that and get off unpunished?' said Mike coldly, and seating himself on the bunk he pulled a dumbstruck Hilly across his knee. 'Someone should have done this a long time ago,' he added, tugging the flimsy skirt up to her waist.

'What? Get off, you can't surely...' Realisation dawned, and Hilly struggled vainly to escape his iron grip.

'Don't worry, your virtue's safe, I'm just going to spank the living daylights out of you,' he continued, pinning her wrists behind her back and trapping her flailing legs with a booted foot.

'Oh no,' Hilly wailed as he felt her knickers being dragged to her knees, then, '*No!*' even louder as a hard hand descended on her pert bottom.

This was no lover's spanking, no subtle arousal gradually building in intensity, punctuated with caresses. Mike was giving vent to a righteous anger and Hilly could expect no mercy.

Nor, Hilly knew, despite her cries and wails, did she deserve any. He was right; she clearly lacked self-discipline and someone really should have exercised control over her earlier. Mike spanked long and hard until all his anger was spent. Sobbing animatedly, her face a mess of tears and make-up, her bottom and thighs a throbbing mass of crimson, Hilly at last managed to force out a single word.

'Sorry,' she whimpered.

Wordlessly he gathered her, dishevelled and wincing, into his arms. 'Apology accepted,' he replied without rancour. He held her close for several minutes and she felt strangely relieved, almost peaceful and, when at last Mike said, 'Now let's get you home,' disappointed.

During the drive Hilly plucked up courage and spoke again. 'How long have you being doing this?'

'Three years. I worked my way through college by driving trucks.' He caught her look of astonishment. 'Didn't expect that, did you? Had us all stereotyped as uneducated and hairy-arsed.'

'Where are you going?' she said, ignoring the truth of what he said.

'Haddons, a clothing manufacturer a few miles from here. You've probably not heard of them.'

'Oh, I have,' said Hilly quietly. 'It's my dad's firm.'

'So, I've just talked my way out of a job,' said Mike heavily as they drew up outside Hilly's flat.

'No really, I won't say a word,' she said fervently, 'I promise.' Suddenly it seemed vitally important not to lose contact.

'We'll see,' he said, jumping down and walking round to the passenger side and lifting her effortlessly down onto the pavement.

'Won't you come in?' she asked hopefully.

'I don't think parking this here will win you any friends with the neighbours,' Mike laughed ironically. 'No, I need my sleep.'

He was just a few miles from home when the phone rang.

'Yeah, it's Mike. What? Go straight on and deliver tonight. Well of course I don't bloody well sound thrilled. Yes, okay.'

An hour later he swung into Haddons' strangely deserted warehouse. If this delivery was so dammed urgent where the hell was everyone? Not wanting to waste any more overdue rest time Mike reversed onto the loading bay, opened the trailer doors and waited, half-dozing, in his cab.

The sound of footsteps stirred him back to consciousness. In his rear-view mirror he watched a figure approach the rear of the truck and remove a small package from the pile of boxes inside. Something about the way they looked, the way they moved, wasn't right. Puzzled and weary, he got out and walked to the back of the vehicle where, for the first time since their momentous encounter a month previously, he met Hilly.

'You!' he snapped crossly. 'You've brought me on this wild goose chase. What is this, some sort of revenge? I was amazed not to get the sack before, but it looks as if you've found some other way to fit me up.'

'Don't jump to conclusions, Mike,' Hilly replied quickly. 'Yes, I did arrange for you to be here, but there was no deception. You really have delivered an important package.'

She flicked back her blonde hair enticingly, the red lipstick smile reminding him of Hilly's manifest physical attractions.

'I've been wanting to meet you again, Mike, to thank you. You did me a favour, not that I thought so at the time...' she patted her bottom ruefully '...being too preoccupied with my hot, sore, little bum.'

'No more than you warranted,' Mike said levelly, discretely aware of how Hilly's tightly-belted raincoat accentuated her narrow waist and enjoying the way she teetered on obviously unaccustomed high heels.

'Quite right, you pulled me up sharp, made me think things through; you're just what this spoilt little rich kid needs, Mike,' she said. 'I hoped perhaps you might feel the same.'

A stirring in his jeans already hinted at the answer, but Mike was cautious. 'I'm not interested in being a plaything.'

'Just what I thought you'd say,' she replied. 'You're probably still angry with me, too. Which is why I had this parcel sent especially from France.' She tore off the wrapping to reveal a bundle of leather thongs firmly attached to a stout wooden handle.

'A whip?' Mike gasped, taken aback.

'A martinet,' Hilly corrected. 'A bastion of French family discipline and still popular with lovers who've a penchant for "*le vice Anglaise*".'

'I think I'm beginning to get the picture,' he said guardedly.

'I got off rather lightly last time, don't you think?' Hilly continued, raising an eyebrow provocatively. 'Perhaps if you were to complete my punishment you might appreciate the sincerity of my desire to get to know you better.'

Mike looked around the warehouse. 'Hardly the best spot.'

'Don't worry, I've already found somewhere more suitable,' Hilly answered. 'Follow me.'

Just who, Mike mused as he followed her through the warehouse and into what in daytime was clearly the manager's office, was calling the shots here? A low-backed chair occupied the centre of the dingy room, and against one wall mounds of papers and a bottle of Jack Daniels topped a battered desk. Tacky girlie calendars, donated free by grateful forklift manufacturers, decorated the walls.

'Drink?' she asked.

Mike shook his head. 'Professional driver,' he pointed out.

'Sorry, silly of me, but I think I'll have a shot.' Hilly poured an inch of the amber fluid into a tumbler. 'Hopefully it has anaesthetic properties,' she said wryly, and downed the liquid in one. Suitably emboldened, she handed Mike the martinet. 'You'll need this,' she added, a tremor in her voice.

'Indeed,' he replied firmly; events were unfolding with

a film-like quality, and for once he was in the lead role instead of the audience.

'And,' she continued briskly, as if to falter for a moment would halt the whole enterprise, 'I'd better remove the coat.' She stood by the chair, slowly and deliberately unknotted the belt and shrugged the raincoat from her shoulders to fall in heap on the floor.

Underneath she wore just a brief blue bra and panties and tautly suspendered, sheer sable-hued stockings. Her legs were long, a counterpoint to voluptuous breasts and hips. Pleasurably aware of his enraptured gaze she stepped forward, bending low over the back of the chair until her head touched the seat. Unbidden, her hands tugged the skimpy little knickers down over her perfect peach of a behind. Daintily she stepped out of them, parted her feet a little for balance and gripped the legs of the chair tightly.

'Okay, Mike, I'm ready,' she said in a fragile voice. 'How many strokes will you give me?'

'As many as I think you deserve,' he replied authoritatively. 'Enough to make every inch of that naughty little bottom hot and sore again.'

'Oh, it's going to hurt,' she moaned, but Mike cut short further complaint with the first swing of the martinet.

He'd never used one before and it took a little experimentation to achieve the desired effect. Holding the handle in his right hand and the tails in his left he gradually adopted a semi-circular action, arcing the biting leather thongs across the curvaceous crown of Hilly's penitently presented rear.

Swit! *Swit*! *Swit*!

Mike alternated from forehand to backhand.

Swit! *Swit*! *Swit*!

Gradually building up a pattern of interwoven, searing lashes that harshly kissed the same areas of chastened flesh again and again.

Hilly was brave, Hilly was stoic – at first. No one individual blow proved unendurable, but after five minutes the cumulative effects were beginning to make themselves painfully felt. The entire landscape of her buttocks and upper thighs throbbed and stung wildly. More disconcertingly this heat seemed, of its own accord, to permeate her abdomen, right to the very depths of her aching sex, and despite her tight grip her lower torso began to gyrate to the rhythm of the whipping. Her derriere thrust up into the air by the high heels, she was sure Mike must have an excellent view of her rapidly moistening quim.

Hilly's guess was correct. The scent and sight of her stimulation were abundantly obvious; likewise the yelps and cries of dismay as Mike made sure she received a thorough thrashing. Every now and again a flailing thong would cruelly cut into the soft white skin at the front of her thighs, adding further decibels to Hilly's already evident distress.

She was at the furthest boundaries of her fortitude. 'Oh Mike,' she pleaded. 'My bottom's on fire. I've been punished enough. Please stop… I'm aching for you.'

'So you think you've earned a respite?' Mike grinned, temporarily laying the martinet aside, the balance of power restored. His fingers unhurriedly traced the slick, sticky lips between Hilly's legs, teasing her labia apart, stroking and squeezing her engorged clitoris.

'Oh yes, oh Mike, I'll do anything you want,' she

47

babbled.

'Anything?' Tantalisingly he slid a single finger into her velvety vulva then, steadying her hips and standing stock still, he rested the tip of his penis at the prominent pink entrance. If Hilly wanted sex she'd have to do the work.

'Oh yes!' Urgently she pushed her buttocks back towards him, anxious to impale her wet sex as deeply as possible on his cock. Still he didn't move. Hampered by her position, Hilly's nylon-sheathed calves visibly strained as she forced her hot quim back onto his rock hard member, twisting her hips, tightly clenching every pelvic muscle to keep him deep inside her, but sensing her approaching climax he abruptly withdrew.

'That's not *fair*,' she complained vehemently, once again denied.

'Life isn't fair, and you'll come when I decide, not a moment before,' Mike declared firmly, jerking Hilly to her feet. He swept the top of the desk clear in a single movement then pushed her roughly across it. Any illusion of control she may have retained vanished; hands pinned into the small of her back by Mike's iron grip she was totally at his mercy.

The martinet flashed down harder than ever, the overlapping blows wheeling her flaming flesh. At once scared and thrilled Hilly meekly pushed her posterior up to meet each scalding stroke, actively inviting the broad leather strips to do their very worst, so sexually charged, so close to fulfilment she was now scarcely aware of the pain.

Eventually, when she thought she could bear the torment no longer, Mike stopped. 'So, you want to come?' he enquired breathlessly.

'Oh please, Mike, screw me,' she gasped. Still holding her firmly down with his left hand Mike's right returned to her saturated sex, slicking the abundant juices from between her nether lips, smearing them over her tight, pouting anus. Hilly gasped as he roughly parted her soundly thrashed buttocks, then again as he began to tease and stroke her virgin rear opening.

'Oh no, Mike, no one's ever… I've never…'

'Be quiet, Hilly.' His voice was commanding, resolute. 'If I take you on it's on my terms. If you want to come I'll decide when and how, and when you need to be punished that's my decision too. This is the last choice I'm offering. Accept the terms or forget it.'

Her bottom blazed, her sex ached for fulfilment and finally she knew clearly what she wanted. 'A-all right…' she whimpered breathlessly.

First a finger carefully invaded the forbidden passage, and a completely new surge of sensual stimulation coursed through her. The tip of Mike's cock pushed against her rear entrance, and she moaned as slowly it distended the ring of muscle, sinking into her, inch by inch. Hilly's bottom was being remorselessly stretched and filled. A moment of panic consumed her: he was too big, she'd never be able to take it all; then suddenly the entire length of his rod was in up to the hilt, his pubic hair rubbed against her burning skin. His cock filled her bottom, the discomfort subsided, and as Mike skilfully finger-fucked her pussy she began once again to push back against him.

He released her wrists, instead employing his free hand to twist and torment her engorged nipples. She gripped the far edge of the table and felt her anus grasp him tightly as he made a final series of powerful, sharp thrusts into her bottom, filling her with his hot, thick sperm.

Her first climax exploded almost instantaneously. The second, her sore buttocks chafed unmercifully on the carpet as Mike returned to fucking her aching pussy, was more languid but every bit as passionate, just as she'd dreamed and imagined so often over the last few weeks; a transport of delight.

Obedience Day

Kate woke to the sound of the radio alarm and lay in bed listening to the announcer's familiar tones: 'Here is the seven o'clock news for Thursday the twenty-forth of April…'

Still only half awake she began the day with a few warming-up exercises, serenaded by the coffee machine bubbling away in the kitchen. Once caffeine had cleared the last of the nighttime cobwebs, she showered then checked her appointment diary, and there in her own neat script she found a most unusual entry: *Obedience Day*.

With a jolt she remembered, and adrenalin coursed through her veins like a surge of electricity. A date selected at random one wine-fuelled evening, a promise to be kept.

Doubt crept in. Would he remember? Could she possibly go through with it? She tried to think logically. True, they'd played similar charades before; but this was the most elaborate, most potentially public yet. Okay, no one was forcing her; a late change of mind wouldn't be catastrophic. Would it? But why settle for a humdrum existence when she had a chance to live on the edge?

The postman interrupted Kate's thoughts, and the sound of the letterbox sent her hurrying to the front door. Excitedly she grabbed envelopes from the mat, anxiously discarding bills in the search for… Yes! Here it was, her master's handwriting on the envelope. Kate read avidly.

Nothing complex at this hour, just a few sartorial details. We shan't meet until this evening but I'll monitor your progress and send further instructions as necessary.

The clothing requirements proved simple enough: some of the scantier and more expensive items from Kate's dress-to-thrill lingerie drawer, stockings instead of the customary tights, a little black dress in place of the usual business suit.

Kate smiled as she read the list. How predictable, she thought, all the usual elements to light a male fire. She balked only at the last edict. High heels were fine for wiggling across the bedroom, or the short walk between taxi and theatre, but for a full day's commuting and office work, no way. She owed it to her toes and calves to compromise and selected a pair with modest, two-inch heels instead.

Forty-five minutes later, chestnut hair shining, discreet makeup impeccable, satchel on her shoulder and season ticket in hand, she entered the metro. The transport authority was having one of its periodic enforcement blitzes and a ticket inspector stood at the barrier. 'Morning, miss,' he said with a brief glance at her pass and a much longer appraisal of her, 'sure you haven't forgotten anything?'

'Not this time,' smiled Kate, confidently boarding the train.

Once at the office the day gradually picked up speed; messages to answer, a creative meeting. Throughout the morning Kate took care to tug down her skirt when sitting lest she treat male colleagues to an indecorous glimpse of stocking. Engrossed in discussion she finally forgot, and then, quickly correcting her posture, saw a good-looking young graphic artist swiftly avert his eyes. When he next looked up Kate held his gaze, her delightful frisson of naughtiness enhanced by his obvious discomfort.

It was lunchtime when a courier brought the flowers. Thankfully Kate was in her own office, high in what had once been the attic of the converted Georgian townhouse. Light, spacious and airy it contained a sofa and drawing board in addition to the usual PC and desk, and took the whole of the roof space. A bit of an extravagance, but what the hell, it was her company.

With the rest of the staff out at lunch, she and a bored young temp in reception were the building's only occupants. Kate was about to reprimand the errant junior for allowing the courier entry when she noticed the card accompanying the bouquet. The motorcycle messenger waited diffidently as she read the message, and as she did Kate felt her chest tighten, and instinctively squeezed her thighs together.

His dusky face creased into a smile as hers reddened. She was mortified; she never blushed. She didn't run her own cutting-edge design company by blushing like a schoolgirl, but clearly the courier already knew more than she'd wanted to reveal and, embarrassed, she blushed even further.

'I've other calls to make, I really must get on,' he told her.

'You know what the card says,' she stated – it wasn't a question.

'Yes,' he replied easily, sitting on the upright chair

before her desk. 'Come here.'

Meekly she obeyed. The wording on the card had, after all, been brief and to the point:

Well really, falling at the first hurdle. Did you think you'd get away with those shoes? Later you'll shop for replacements, but for now Rufus will reprimand you in a rather more direct and effective way.

'Lift your dress, please,' Rufus said softly, and mesmerised like a rabbit caught in the beam of a hunter's torch, she did so.

Of course it wasn't the first time Kate had been draped over a stranger's knee. Not that they were into swapping or swinging or anything so provincially tacky. No, but there are clubs: discrete, urban, upmarket invitation only gatherings for those who love to dress and act up. Monogamy had been agreed with her master from the start; club nights simply simmered a sexual tension they'd later release in private.

Rufus grasped her waist firmly before pushing her dress up clear of the target area. This guy clearly worked out, played a lot of sport, or was no stranger to manual labour. Probably all three, intellectual rough trade – every middle class girl's dream.

'You won't take my knickers down, will you?' she whispered, feeling intensely vulnerable yet desperately aroused. She could feel his muscles – one in particular. What if her colleagues returned early?

'I won't need to,' replied Rufus, tugging the skimpy fabric tightly into her cleft and setting to work.

He was clearly no stranger to the art of spanking, either that, or had done the background reading. Textbook stuff; firm methodical slaps to alternate cheeks soon left no part of her bottom untouched; pauses for a soothing palm to stroke the reddening moons, ears deaf to the entreaties that soon betrayed her initial vow to keep silent.

Five minutes later Rufus stood up, effortlessly lifting Kate's slender frame and setting her onto her feet to watch amused as she stood, hands clutching her blazing bottom, eyes brimming, voice full of emotion.

'Oh, that's so *sore*,' she complained.

'Face the wall, hands on head, no rubbing,' he commanded calmly, and took out a small compact camera.

An hour later the recipient of a series of snapshots would delight at the contrast between coral white silk and crimson skin, for now Rufus had the satisfaction of a job well done. 'I'll let myself out,' he said quietly. 'Your next instruction will come by phone.'

Kate sat at her desk, immediately regretted it, and adjourned chastened and excited to the toilet to repair her make-up and check the rear-end damage in the mirror. Breathing a little less rapidly she returned to the office, shoved the flowers into a vase and reluctantly turned her attention to more mundane matters of business.

But try as she might, Kate couldn't concentrate.

Two hours later very little work had been done and beneath the clinging dress her hot bottom smarted cruelly, a constant reminder of her humiliating ordeal. She fretted. How would she know what to do next if he didn't call? Then suddenly it dawned on her. The phone hadn't rung at all. Furious at herself for being so stupid she buzzed the temp.

'Why haven't I had any calls?' she demanded testily.

'You said not to disturb you,' replied the girl, with sulky self-justification.

'I said no such thing,' retorted Kate.

'No,' agreed the girl, 'not in person, but the courier gave me the message on his way out.'

Kate abandoned the conversation; there was no point in arguing. 'Well, put any calls through immediately from now on, please,' she said, petulantly replacing the receiver. Half an hour before the office closed. In that time two calls made her jump, anxiously grab the phone, struggle to contain her disappointment, then force her voice back to normal and speak with a client. Eventually, with five minutes to go, her habitual bright professionalism reduced to the anxious state of a teenager who suspects she's been stood up on a date, Kate heard his familiar voice at the other end of the line.

'Took you a while to catch on,' he chuckled. 'Now listen carefully. There's a little shop in Poland Street called *Mata Hari*. Go there at once. You'll be served some shoes, further instructions and something to think about. Oh, and Kate, this time just do as you're told.'

With a click he was gone, and the only word she'd got in edgeways was a slur on his parentage. Fortunately her anger gradually dissipated to be replaced by a buzz of anticipation as she made the short walk through the teeming city streets.

The sign on the door of *Mata Hari* told Kate it was closed, but she had now at least grasped the rudiments of this game, and knocked firmly on the glass panel. After a brief rattle of bolts the door opened and in she went.

The shop had something of a reputation. Situated in a

back street in a previously rundown but now trendy part of town the shop was owned by the son and daughter of an *enfant terrible* designer of the 1960's. Its stock in trade was exotica; a narrow, and pricey, niche market, where fetish wear, original '50's and '60's glamour and modern fashion merged to produce the sort of look beloved of style magazine art editors.

Since this was Kate's maiden visit she stopped for a moment to take in the surroundings. Original 'New Look' dresses scrounged from the flea markets of Europe vied for attention with perspex-heeled fluffy mules and less easily identifiable items in shiny PVC; a clothing cornucopia.

'Have a seat,' said the young assistant who'd let her in. 'Can I get you a drink – some red wine?'

'Please, but no alcohol, some fizzy water perhaps,' replied Kate, who'd no desire to blur her senses. Right now reality was thrilling enough.

'No problem.' The assistant disappeared towards the back of the shop and Kate continued her look around. She was admiring a beautiful, full-length 1950's cocktail dress when the floorwalker returned, glass in hand.

'Beautiful, isn't it?' she smiled. 'I've been admiring it for weeks, but,' she added, a note of prompting in her American-accented voice, 'it's shoes you've come for.'

'That's right,' Kate confirmed, sitting down. 'I believe some have been put aside for me?'

'Indeed,' agreed the girl, 'he was very specific… Very good-looking, too,' she added with a mischievous smile. 'All the same, I think I'd better check the fit. My name's Jo Jo, by the way.' Fetching a box from the counter she crouched at Kate's feet to remove her existing footwear, motioning her back into the chair with a wave of her hand when she leant forward to help.

'That's my job,' she said resolutely, but repeating her earlier smile she slipped Kate's trim feet into the new shoes with practised skill. From her brief survey of the shop's stock Kate had been in some trepidation as to what to expect: Westwood platforms, dominatrix spike heels? Instead, to her relief, she was fitted with a variation on the theme of classic black courts, in beautiful soft leather with a square heel and single, elegant strap across the instep.

Jo Jo's hands lingered, tentatively tracing the contours of Kate's slim nylon-covered right calf, following the outline of gym-toned muscles, fingers softly sliding up towards her knee, and just beyond. Her sensual touch sent a shiver of guilty desire through Kate, who sighed, parting her legs a fraction, mutely permitting the girl's tentative caresses.

'You've gorgeous legs,' said Jo Jo, with such evident sincerity that Kate for the first time observed her closely. Dusky skin and a pretty face, with features that were hard to pin down. If she was mixed race she got the best of all worlds, thought Kate wryly. Pale lipstick was the only sign of make-up. She had dark shoulder-length tresses, several silver rings in each ear and a stud on one side of her nose. Her white sleeveless T-shirt outlined firm, small breasts. An intricate tattoo circled each upper arm, the edge of another just visible at the top of her cleavage. She had a narrow waist to die for, tight leather miniskirt and bare legs, every bit as stunning as Kate's. Short white socks and fashionably strappy platform sandals completed the cheeky ensemble.

Looking down, Kate enjoyed the voyeuristic pleasure of viewing the small triangle of white between Jo Jo's thighs, and felt her own sex dampen as the girl's hand slid even higher, stroking the naked skin of her upper thigh. Then, abruptly, Jo Jo stood, holding out a hand to help Kate to her feet. 'You'd better try walking in them,' she said, as if the last few minutes had never happened.

Nonplussed, but aware the change of demeanour was deliberately intended to throw her, Kate took an experimental trip around the shop floor and found the shoes surprisingly comfortable, despite the change they made to her posture; pushing her bottom out and forcing her to draw back her shoulders in order to remain poised and balanced.

'They look good,' said the girl. 'I helped him choose,' she added with a grin.

'Thank you, how much…?' began Kate.

'Oh no, the financial side's sorted…' explained the girl, then without a pause again adroitly changed subject in mid-sentence, '…but you realise I'll have to punish you?'

'Punish me?' gasped Kate. 'But I've already been—'

'Spanked, yes I know,' the girl cut in. 'By the courier, lucky you.'

'Then why—?'

'Because you're arguing with me, for a start. And because of your rudeness; your master says to tell you his parents were definitely married when he was born.'

Kate ruefully remembered her ill-advised telephone insult and his subsequent threat.

'Come here,' commanded Jo Jo, 'Time's passing and I don't want you missing your train.' She led Kate towards a large mirror. 'Stand here, hands above your head and lean forward until they touch the wall, and take the weight on your palms and the balls of your feet.

'It'll make a change to dish it out for once,' Jo Jo added enigmatically, lifting Kate's dress to her waist. 'Now, much as I relish the prospect of smacking that cute little ass with my bare hands, these rings on my fingers might cause more damage than we bargained for. So fortunately I have an inflexible friend to assist me in our little sister to sister encounter.'

Looking round, Kate bit her lip at the discovery that the 'friend' took the form of a wooden hairbrush, then inhaled sharply as Jo Jo yanked her knickers down to her knees.

'Hmm,' observed her tormentor, 'things are getting a little hot and damp down there, I see. I guess in your position my pussy would be sending the same messages.'

And then Kate's ordeal began. Her strained stance, aided by Jo Jo's hand on her abdomen, positioned Kate's pert posterior perfectly. Her tormentor kept up a steady rhythm, allowing just sufficient time between each expert flick of the wrist for the smart of the previous impact to be fully absorbed. Gradually Kate's bottom turned bright, blush-red as the hard wooden back of the brush hit the same spot a second and even third time. Stealthily Jo Jo's hand slid downwards until her fingers touched Kate's pubic mound, every subsequent smack forcing her throbbing sex closer to these discrete explorations. The muscles on her calves and thighs tightened as her hips writhed between pain and pleasure. Gasping and moaning at the conflicting sensations pulsing through her lower body Kate's movements began to lewdly echo those of more conventional sex; pushing out her burning buttocks to meet the next punishing collision then forcing her loins forward to feel the glorious touch of the shop assistant's expert fingers.

'Oh…' whimpered Kate, somewhere between agony and ecstasy. 'Oh, that hurts… oh yes, my clit, oh don't stop, please…'

'Go for it, girl; give in to the feeling,' cajoled Jo Jo. 'Let yourself come, you've been wanting this ever since that courier had you over his lap.'

The memory of Rufus belabouring her poor sore bottom finally did it and with one great shuddering gasp Kate came. Her knees went weak and, but for Jo Jo's surprisingly strong grasp, she'd have sunk in a heap on the floor.

'Boy, you make a noise,' laughed the stunning Eurasian. 'I didn't make half so much fuss when my guy whipped me last night.'

'You get punished as well?' Kate asked, taken aback.

'Don't be fooled by the piercing and tattoos,' revealed Jo Jo. 'I'm usually sub, not that seeing to you hasn't made a girl quite hot and bothered,' she added. 'Typically though, I'm in your predicament, look,' she turned, tugged up her skirt and pulled aside plain white cotton knickers to reveal a behind liberally striped with red weals.

'One jolly good hiding, as you Brits say.' She shivered at the memory. 'Mind you, it was worth it; he screwed me senseless afterwards.'

Kate laughed, partly in solidarity, partly pleasure at Jo Jo's uncomplicated acceptance of her sexuality. Then a car horn sounded outside.

'Woops, get your stuff together, that's your cab to the station.' Jo Jo steered Kate towards the door.

'B-but,' Kate stammered, 'where am I going?'

'To the station, miss?' the cabby asked rhetorically, and flustered and bewildered, Kate was on her way. 'You'll just about be in time,' he added, skilfully threading his way through the early evening traffic.

'But I haven't a ticket, and I don't even know where I'm going,' Kate complained.

Without taking his eyes from the road the cabby reached back and handed her an envelope. 'One single to Oxford,' he said brusquely. 'A car will take you on to Melton Towers.'

Melton Towers; the name was familiar. Yes, now Kate remembered, you could see it from the main line, a large Georgian pile a few miles beyond Oxford – the town where she'd attended university.

The cab stopped at the terminus, and Kate was suddenly aware that the chances of her being away overnight with nothing more then the contents of her handbag were growing by the minute. 'How much…?'

'All taken care of.' Scarcely had she alighted when the taxi was off, one of a host of identical black cabs jockeying for space in heavy traffic.

Hurrying across the platform Kate caught the Oxford train with two minutes to spare. The coaches were curiously old-fashioned, like those remembered from childhood holidays with a single corridor along one side with compartments leading off. Each had a sliding door and plump moquette covered bench seats facing fore and aft, luggage racks above them. Posters featuring watercolour images of '30's seaside resorts hung on the walls, and thick leather straps fastened wooden sash windows.

Despite the rush of late homebound commuters, Kate found an empty corner and settled in, grateful for the chance to collect her thoughts. While the train clattered across the suburbs and out into open countryside she produced a compact and refreshed her make-up, and looking at herself in the mirror she blushed at the memory of how sexually abandoned she'd so recently been – and with another female…

A knock on the door made her look up with a start. 'Sorry to make you jump, miss,' said a pleasant voice. 'May I see your ticket, please?'

Kate returned his smile and reached for her bag. 'Hang on,' she said, 'haven't I seen you somewhere before?'

'Shouldn't think so,' said the uniformed man. 'Not unless you travelled up to town on this line this morning.'

'No, I didn't, I must be mistaken,' Kate replied, but as she handed over the ticket the half-remembered image suddenly clicked into focus. This morning, the ticket inspector. But how…?

She was just about to pose the question when he stared at her and spoke sternly. 'I'm sorry, miss, but this is the wrong ticket.'

'Wrong ticket?' Kate was taken aback. 'But it's a single to Oxford, with today's date. How can it be incorrect?'

'Because you're going to Melton.'

How could he know? Hang on, one step at a time. 'Yes, by car from Oxford.'

'No, the train's stopping at Melton.'

'But this service doesn't stop at Melton.' Kate was wondering what on earth was going on.

'Not normally, no,' confirmed the inspector. 'But it will today. And since that's your destination you need a ticket to Melton not Oxford.'

'But Melton's nearer than Oxford, so the journey's paid for anyway, so what difference does it make?'

'No need to get angry, miss.' The inspector was implacable. 'By not producing the correct ticket you've broken the law. Magistrates and a hefty fine, I should think.'

'Look, I didn't even buy the ticket – you can't punish me for something I haven't...' Kate paused for a moment, realisation dawning. 'But you can, can't you? That's what this little melodrama's all about. A neat little set-up to ensure my comeuppance.'

'Awfully astute of you, miss,' smiled the inspector. 'Absolutely right. As it happens, there's an alternative penalty, subject to you obeying my instructions to the letter.'

'And it was you at the tube this morning,' Kate continued, barely acknowledging the official's statement, 'which is how someone else knew about the shoes...'

'A very bright girl indeed,' nodded the inspector, somewhat patronisingly. 'But if we might conclude the immediate business before we reach Melton.'

Kate hesitated for a moment, and then slowly nodded. 'I – I think I can guess what's involved.'

'Excellent, sensible as well as intelligent.' The inspector quickly shut the sliding door prior to drawing the blinds. 'Pity there's no lock, but we'll just have to hope no one comes in,' he observed.

'Now,' he turned to face her, his manner once more authoritarian, his voice frosty, 'kneel on the seat and hitch your skirt up, if you please.'

With the sinking feeling that her instinct had been correct, Kate did so.

'Reach up and grasp the luggage rack,' he ordered. Again she complied, acutely aware that the position thrust her barely covered buttocks prominently before him. Silently the inspector fastened the hem of her skirt clear of her hips with a safety-pin and pulled her knickers down to rest tangled about her knees.

'Mm, a peach of a bottom,' he observed, delicately running his hands over the two globes, 'and already dealt with today, if I'm not mistaken.'

Gritting her teeth, Kate was annoyed to discover her body unilaterally responding to the touch of his warm hands, then risking a glance over her shoulder she glimpsed him remove the well-worn strap from the window, bend it back and forth, and slap the leather experimentally against his palm.

'A dozen strokes with this beauty should teach you not to cheat the railways,' he said grimly. 'Protest loud enough and you'll probably have passengers running to your aid, if you don't mind being found in such an embarrassing position, of course.'

Arms raised above her head, bottom bared and defenceless, at once scared and thrilled at the prospect of her poor backside enduring its third chastisement of the day, Kate's reply was succinct if not overly subtle. 'Just get on with it,' she whispered.

Not one to disappoint a lady, the inspector did so, laying on six steady stokes, alternating from forehand to back, broad stripes of carefully gauged penance evidence of his determination to tame the shrew.

Kate gasped and squirmed as her bare backside was methodically beaten. Inevitably the initial smart became a deep-seated glow, and with another need now uppermost in her mind she began to push her yearning sex against the coarse fabric of the seatback. Making no concessions to modesty or appearance, deaf to her own impassioned moans, she felt a familiar dampness and arousal spread through her loins, and was on the brink of an orgasm when the inspector intervened.

'Quite enough of that miss, thank you,' he admonished crossly. 'We'll have no such dissolute behaviour, if you please.'

Taking a step back he swung the strap further and harder, cutting diagonally across the earlier stripes; another half dozen, pain upon pain. The last, low down across her thighs, ensured the entire surface of her buttocks blazed with heat and discomfort, and the prospect of ever again sitting comfortably seemed remote. Grinding her hips against the cushions no longer bought comfort and, most humiliating of all, Kate felt tears in her eyes. Then she noticed the train slowing down, the rhythmic clatter changing tempo, steel screeching on steel as the brakes were applied.

'Ah, Melton, your stop.' The inspector's voice was once again congenial. 'Let me assist you, miss.' Her knickers were pulled up, feeling strangely tight and chafing against her punished skin, and then he helped her stumble to her feet.

'Don't forget your bag, miss,' the inspector smiled, carefully taking her by the elbow, across the corridor and off the train. 'Thank for travelling with us, we do hope to see you again.'

Bewildered and angry Kate stood on the deserted platform, surreptitiously massaging her sore bottom through the fabric of her skirt. Then a whistle sounded and the train disappeared into the distance.

Walking gingerly towards the exit, still warily rubbing her ravaged rear, she was not altogether surprised to discover a large car waiting, a familiar leather clad figure standing beside it, and bowing gracefully he opened the rear door of the limousine. Kate climbed in appreciatively, wincing as she sat, despite the luxury of cool leather upholstery.

Carefully negotiating the narrow country lanes the chauffeur watched Kate shift restlessly in his mirror, soreness and frustration doing nothing to improve her mood.

'I can see you aren't sitting comfortably,' he said at length, but received no reply. 'I'll take that silent glare as confirmation,' Rufus continued, unruffled. 'Don't worry, I've something here that may help.' Halting in a lay-by he reached into the glove compartment, and a moment later he was sitting next to Kate on the capacious rear seat, stretching his legs across the deep pile carpet. 'Let me help,' he suggested, drawing her down across his lap.

Kate remained on her guard. 'Oh no, you're not going to give me another hiding,' she gasped, her body stiffening.

'Relax,' Rufus reassured, pushing down on her shoulders and lifting her skirt, 'let's check the damage.' Resigned to her knickers coming down yet again, Kate meekly lifted her hips to assist his task.

'Oh dear, oh dear,' he murmured reprovingly, 'the inspector did get carried away.' He tentatively stroked the crimson flesh. Flinching at first, Kate sighed deeply as his expert hands began to massage cold cream into her scalded skin. Moaning contentedly she pushed her pubis against his muscular leather clad thighs, letting his hands sooth away the pain, just what she'd dreamed of since last encountering this very model of a desirable male.

Blissful minutes passed and Kate's breathing began to deepen in response to Rufus's adeptly probing fingers, which occasionally strayed, as if by accident, into her moist cleft, then delicately caressed her sensitive inner thighs. Kate's sexuality took over, her hips undulating urgently as she moved to attain the release forbidden her on the train.

'On no,' intoned Rufus, firmly bursting the bubble. 'Much as I'd delight in making you come, that's the master's prerogative. You'll have to wait a little longer, I'm afraid.'

He returned to the driver's seat leaving Kate, comforted but unsatisfied, struggling to contain her disappointment, but fortunately she'd little time to ponder this latest denial, for within minutes they reached Melton Towers, where Kate was welcomed by yet another familiar face.

'Jo Jo!' she exclaimed, her tone a mixture of surprise and pleasure.

'Welcome, madam,' the maid's tone made it clear they must keep to their allotted roles, but the twinkle in her eye revived Kate's spirits immediately. 'I'll show you to your room; you've an hour to shower and change before meeting the master at dinner.'

Kate followed Jo Jo through the imposing portico and up a grand staircase flanked with portraits of nineteenth century family retainers. She led Kate to an enormous room, dominated by a four-poster bed and bay windows with a view across acres of carefully manicured gardens.

'Drink first, then shower and change,' said Jo Jo briskly and Kate, almost overwhelmed by the day's events, was only too happy to agree.

Savouring a large gin and tonic she admired the view while Jo Jo busied herself in the bathroom, and it wasn't until she felt fingers carefully unzipping her dress that Kate realised she'd returned.

'Time to get you ready,' the girl whispered in her ear.

With practiced ease Jo Jo slipped Kate's clothes from her body. First her dress, then bra. Kate's nipples hardened as, all too briefly, Jo Jo cupped a breast in each hand. 'So beautiful,' she said softly.

Knickers, suspender belt, stockings and shoes joined the heap on the floor, and finally Jo Jo led her unprotesting and naked to the shower, staying her hand as Kate reached automatically for the soap. 'No, let me do the work,' she said. 'You just get yourself in the right frame of mind to meet the master.'

Kate let the hot water flow over her, easing the day's discomforts and surrendering to Jo Jo's skilful ministrations. After first washing her hair the servant set to work with a bar of soap, covering every inch of Kate's body with a creamy lather before carefully rinsing her off. As Jo Jo's hands roamed over her breasts and across her flat stomach Kate felt her desire rise yet again, and this time she determined not to be thwarted. Without warning she pulled Jo Jo fully-clothed into the shower, wrapped her arms tightly around her and kissed her hard on the mouth.

Jo Jo's response was just as passionate, forcing her tongue between Kate's lips, simultaneously sliding a finger deep into her willing sex.

Hungrily they kissed, drenched with water, bodies intertwined. Urgently Kate prised a hand between Jo Jo's legs, pushing her thighs apart, fingers sliding into her knickers to find her clitoris, and together they reached a mutual climax.

Gasping, Jo Jo switched off the shower. 'Oh wow,' she sighed, 'that definitely wasn't in the plan. I'm going to get my bottom well and truly tanned for that little lapse.'

'But worth it?' Still washed by waves of intense pleasure Kate grinned conspiratorially.

'Oh yes, well worth it,' Jo Jo fervently insisted. 'If I can recall that while I get my rump reddened later there'll certainly be a second coming.

'Listen,' she continued, 'I was supposed to help you dress but water marks won't make you belle of the ball. You'll find everything you need laid out on the bed, okay?'

'I'll be fine,' Kate smiled happily. 'I'm now ready to face the world. Thank you, Jo Jo, I do hope I haven't got you into too much trouble.'

'No more than I signed up for,' the girl replied easily. 'Enjoy the evening,' and she was gone, leaving only a trail of damp footprints.

Dried and scented Kate examined the evening attire laid out for her. The discovery of the beautiful, off-the-shoulder '50's party dress she'd so admired in *Mata Hari* was hardly a bombshell. A black basque, sheer black stockings and high-heeled sandals, all from the same era, completed the look, and no doubt the absence of any panties was deliberate.

Carefully fastening the basque, Kate felt it tightly cinch her waist, flattered by the way it thrust her bosom into prominence. Languorously she rolled up each expensive stocking, carefully fastening the suspender clips, taking care to keep each seam straight. Then the dress, and she nodded approvingly at her reflection in the mirror and concluded her careful preparations by slipping on the shoes and applying red lipstick. Then, suppressing the butterflies in her stomach, she took a deep breath and headed out of the bedroom.

Dinner was served in the dining room, capacious and full of interesting furniture, *objets d'art* and acres of books, and combinations of candles and up lighters providing a warm surrounding glow.

The master greeted Kate with a kiss and warm embrace, seating her at a table set with beautiful bone china and antique silver cutlery. No servants intervened to interrupt them; instead they served themselves with simple but delicious food from heated tureens. 'More intimate this way,' the master confided, refilling her wine glass.

'Time for some edited highlights of your day,' he smiled, drawing her attention to a large video screen in one corner.

'You filmed everything?' Kate gasped.

'Not me, Sir Ronald,' the master replied, amused. Kate

looked blank. 'Chairman of the train company, owner of this property, amateur film buff, and committed voyeur...' he continued. 'In return for his participation – the ticket inspector – he put an awful lot of facilities at my disposal.'

'You mean...?'

'Exactly. Those who shared your adventures were not only in on the secret but were, you might say, likeminded folk. I even had a bit-part myself; driving that cab was rather fun.' Surprise rendered Kate momentarily speechless.

'For example, if I can remember how to operate this thing, Rufus and Jo Jo... ah yes.' An image appeared on the blank blue screen, and Kate watched in amazement as Jo Jo, in the maid uniform, was bent over a kitchen table, skirt up, knickers nowhere to be seen and her bottom showing the signs of a recent chastisement. Behind her Rufus tossed aside a large wooden spoon and reached for the zip of his leather trousers. Jo Jo visibly shuddered with delight as he slipped his long hard length into her and began to pound his pelvis against her burning cheeks. Kate let out an involuntary groan of envy at the sight of her new friend being well and truly seen to in the servant's quarters, and she flushed, her face red, her sex hotter.

'Yes, I thought that might appeal,' observed the master. 'As you can see, they are clearly enthusiastic CP devotees.'

For the next twenty minutes Kate was treated to an alternative perspective on her recent trials and tribulations. She said nothing, fully engaged by the replay: Rufus taking her across his knee in the office, the events at *Mata Hari*, the ticket inspector, even the shower scene of little more than an hour before.

'A most arousing sequence of incidents,' concluded the master with customary understatement. 'You've proved neither especially obedient nor,' he paused to rewind Jo Jo and Kate's shower room escapade, 'able to resist temptation.'

There was no point in arguing, and besides, Kate realised with a deliciously dangerous feeling of fatalistic anticipation, she didn't care.

Over the course of a single day each of her senses had been stretched to the limit, her erotic imagination stimulated further than she could ever have envisioned. Now she felt tranquil, ready to offer herself up to whatever her master might wish. Anything was permissible.

Apparently intuitively possessed of this knowledge, but then after all, that's why he was the master, he rose from his chair, grasped her shoulders and gazed unblinkingly into her eyes. 'It's time for your final trial and ultimate reward. I expect you to remain trusting, obedient and submissive throughout.' He smiled an ironic smile. 'Either way, you will be punished.' As he spoke he pulled a velvet blindfold from his pocket and brought sudden darkness to Kate's world, heightening her senses of sound and touch. Then, taking her hand he guided her towards the stairs.

'Place your hands behind your back, walk before me and listen carefully to my directions.' Sedate and composed Kate stepped into the unknown. Her heels clicked across the marble hall as she strained to catch his whispered commands.

'Turn right, steps going up.' Across parquet then rugs, Kate experienced the size of the rooms by the changes in temperature and the echo of her footsteps. At last the smell of fabric and a thick rug underfoot indicated a bedroom. She heard the door click shut behind them and the master's stealthy approach, Kate remained motionless as her dress was undone and slid to her feet. 'Step forward and raise your hands,' he instructed. Just within the upward limit of her reach was a horizontal wooden bar, suspended from two ropes, and unseeing she instinctively grasped the trapeze-like fixture. The ritual was about to begin.

He left her alone on tiptoe for several minutes. Was she to be whipped? How perversely might she yet be required to please him?

The impact of a hand on her buttocks returned Kate to reality with a jolt. He spanked her laconically, almost tenderly, causing little more than a mild stinging heat and roseate blush. Inwardly, her libido in turmoil, Kate's carnal desires grew apace. Experience told her this was merely a salacious preamble to the main event.

A yearning in her belly ached to be filled and Kate wantonly began to rotate her hips in mute invitation. The master's methodical disciplining of her peachy globes continued regardless then, just when Kate felt she could endure her sensual torment no longer, the spanking ceased.

'Spread your legs wide,' he commanded, gripping Kate's hips and sinking to his knees before her. Revelling in the sinful sight she knew she must present she needed no further urging to obey. His hands moved to the apex of her parted thighs, adroit fingers stroked her swollen clitoris, and a tongue probed deep between her quivering labia. Saturated by flowing juices she writhed and groaned, unable to resist his sensual mastery and swept by waves of pleasure she surrendered to an explosive orgasm.

Elegantly he stood, lips wet with her outpourings, to gently loosen her white-knuckled grip on the bar. Effortlessly the master cradled her in his arms and carried her limp form to the *chaise longue* where he removed the now redundant blindfold. Blinking against the dim light Kate looked up, studying his expression; kindness steeled with a hint of cruelty. Unresisting she lay on her back, allowed her master to pull her knees up to her chest, and expose her fully to his gaze.

'Your final reward,' he whispered softly. 'The crop. You'll mark well.'

With perfect aim the tip flicked across her burnished bottom, sought out the pale unmarked flesh of her inner thighs, came within a whisper of her sopping sex. Kate moaned and squirmed but made no effort to escape. Gratefully relinquishing her body to his dominion, excited beyond mere pain or pleasure, wanting only the paramount sensation of deep unrelenting penetration – hard and fast and soon.

He stopped, but she felt only abandonment and not relief. 'More,' Kate distantly heard her voice cry. 'Please master, I need more.'

Again the crop whistled through the air, employing its full length across the raw soreness of her welted bottom, and then he urgently knelt before her on the *chaise*, wrestled off his clothes, kissed her neck, face and hair, lifted her calves into the air and with one ardent thrust shafted Kate to the hilt… and ever obedient she timed her coming with his.

Kate stirred, slowly waking from deep peaceful sleep to the sound of the radio alarm announcing a new morning. Her lower body ached mysteriously, but she felt good.

'Here is the seven o'clock news for Thursday the twenty-forth of April…'

Kate struggled to remember. She was sure there was something special about the coming day…

Party Conference

Far from the noisy crowds and smoky rooms of the party conference, Josephine was glad of a respite from the politicians who'd once again taken over this fashionable southern seaside resort for their annual bash. She needed to walk and she needed to think, somewhere quiet, away from the braying hoards. Her concerns were predominantly personal, not political, but a decade as an MP's wife had taught her the two were often inextricably connected.

She'd tried to ignore the doubts but her uneasiness persisted, worsened by a week's enforced social contact with braying party stalwarts. Henry had been one of the lucky few to retain his seat at the last election so in theory life could continue as normal, albeit in opposition. But Josephine, unlike the depleted ranks of backbenchers, no longer wanted the status quo.

In any case the once great party, seemingly electorially unassailable for so long, had now split, perhaps irrevocably, into hundreds of squabbling factions, all hell-bent on arguing the toss over obscure ideological points and apparently oblivious to the fact that the world had moved on. Even now, over two years on, a large section of members still seemed unable to accept the realities of defeat; it was the fault of the EU for destroying national unity, gays and feminists for undermining the family, the fault of anybody and everybody but a group of ageing white males who'd failed to keep up with the changes in social attitudes. Which, Josephine had to admit, included her dinosaur of a husband. The party had turned right, but the country, Great Britain plc, had gone straight on.

At length the pale autumn sunshine waned and she abandoned her bracing walk along the promenade in search of warmth and a reviving cup of coffee. The town's cafés were packed to the gunnels with media types and *apparatchiks* and Josephine was fortunate even to find a table to share.

Opposite her sat a man in his thirties; slim, good-looking and informally dressed in black jeans, check shirt, and a fleece jacket, and Henry's likely reaction came to mind: 'Huh, fella's got an earring – must be gay.' Well, sod Henry; Josephine craved convivial conversation.

And luck was on her side, for the young man – Mark, she quickly discovered – was happy to chat and reluctantly in town for the conference too.

'Not really my area, politics,' he admitted ruefully. 'But my paper wanted a feature on life behind the scenes, the human angle, loyal servants, "those who serve" and all that. 'No, you're quite safe,' he added, sensing her caution. 'I've not got my notebook out, or my tape recorder on.' He turned out empty pockets to illustrate his sincerity. 'Actually,' he confided with a mischievous grin she found appealing, 'I'm skiving off to a photographic exhibition this afternoon.'

'What a coincidence!' Josephine exclaimed, and almost before she knew it her story spilled out. 'You see, before Henry – the honourable member for Essex South – swept me off my naïve nineteen-year-old feet at a young member's dance, I'd begun a photographic degree. But sadly I never completed the course. Encouraged by my parents, who thoroughly approved the match with Henry – they thought his family socially superior and couldn't see the point of an arts subject anyway – I foolishly abandoned my studies to become his pretty little wife.' Her voice heavy with regret, Josephine continued, 'I meant to go back to college but two daughters followed in rapid succession and Henry's job came first as he rose without trace to a minor cabinet post. Feminism's a dirty word in our party, so I gritted my teeth, did what was expected and got on with the hearth and home routine. The children occupied most of my time until Henry decided boarding school would be best – although I'm not sure for whom.

'Then, typically, after numerous public speeches stating how important it was to families that women should stay at home and not work, Henry decreed I should have a "real job" as his appointments secretary. The Commons paid a generous salary so, as he'd now the flat in town and our constituency house to support, it would be prudent, he was sure I'd agree.'

Josephine became uncomfortably aware that she'd spent the last ten minutes telling a complete stranger the story of her life, but fortunately he didn't seem to mind, displaying a refreshing ability to listen instead of cutting in with his own anecdotes as Henry usually did.

'A photographer,' he said. 'Well then, I'd welcome your opinion. Come to the exhibition with me.'

Just like that, unplanned spontaneity. An attractive guy wanted the company of a bored politician's wife. Somewhat taken aback Josephine was about to explain that she couldn't possibly, when she recalled a former PM's exhortations on the importance of choice. Quite.

The gallery was small and select and initially Josephine felt out of place, but Mark knew the owner and they soon became engrossed in the works; images of sexual fantasy and submission abounded, many suggesting their subject's willing participation.

Fortunately Josephine wasn't an instinctive prude; some newspapers might fulminate and condemn but she was sufficiently educated to appreciate the artistic merit enough to sense the erotic power. Lingering over some prints Josephine sensed long dormant sexual passions stir within her. She felt herself dampen and discreetly clenched her thighs to accentuate the unaccustomed physical pleasure.

'Great, aren't they?' said Mark, taking her arm intimately. 'Ever take any pictures like this?'

'I worked in black and white, certainly, but nothing so daring.' Josephine was amazed; a proper conversation about art, indirectly about sex, without sniggering or condescension; someone who assumed she might have some competence with a camera.

'I've got a couple of books and magazines of documentary stuff back at the hotel,' Mark went on. 'If you're not busy this evening perhaps you like to see them?'

'Unfortunately I am.' She felt a sharp pang of regret. 'There's a fringe meeting and Henry will expect my presence on his arm. Actually, after five minutes or so he probably wouldn't notice if a chandelier fell on my head. His eager-beaver researcher will, however, no doubt be present to advise him throughout the evening,' she added sarcastically.

'A researcher?' Mark enquired mildly, sensing more to come.

'Oh, I'm not a complete fool,' she continued. 'The late votes and the "sorry old thing, urgent meeting up in town" excuses are doubtless sometimes true, but I know in my heart his pretty young Cambridge-educated employee is assisting him with more than white papers. Not that it won't rebound on the deluded fool in the long run; does he really think a young graduate nearly half his age desires anything more than a shortcut up the career ladder? However, I'm afraid tonight I'm supposed to be on duty.'

Mark's look of disappointment seemed so sincere it triggered within Josephine a ridiculous thought; he didn't fancy her, did he? The sudden certainty that should such a crazy idea turn out to be true prompted another impromptu decision – the second in as many hours. What a day this was turning out to be.

'But then, on second thoughts, a diplomatic headache should do the trick,' she dared to say. 'Yes, thank you Mark, that would be nice. Which hotel are you staying at?'

Her prediction proved correct, a few muttered words of unconvincing sympathy and Henry appeared more than happy to go off and entertain the backwoodsmen on his own. Josephine dallied, apprehensive and excited. She stood in front of the mirror trying with little success to soften her regulation hairstyle. Goodness, she was as nervous as a teenager dressing up for a date, and totally out of practice.

At least, the reflection reassured her, her regime of sit-ups and horse riding had maintained a commendably trim figure. Nervously she applied more make-up than usual, chose a lipstick a little less pale. Such minor, unpractised alterations did little to alter the stockbroker-belt look, but what the hell, at last she'd something to look forward too. Feeling more excited at the prospect of new company than she could remember, Josephine set boldly out.

Mark was a charming and considerate host and the evening proved as special as Josephine had hoped. He poured wine, listened attentively and frequently asked her views. His photographic books were every bit as good as promised, and browsing avidly Josephine caught sight of a couple of magazines casually left on a low table. Mark watched expectantly as she picked them up, minutes passed, and at last Josephine broke the tense silence.

'Did you expect I'd be shocked?' she enquired.

'Yes,' he replied frankly.

'Sorry, I'm not,' she confided.

'You find them arousing?' Mark asked, straightforward as always.

'Yes,' Josephine admitted. 'I've no direct experience and as for my fantasies, well, I find them much harder to speak of candidly than you. I missed out on the supposedly liberating experience of hippies and free love, and your generation is so much more matter-of-fact about things sexual. But, since it appears to be implicit in your question, I've wondered what it would be like to be mastered by someone I could trust. You know, forced into erotic adventures against my will, that sort of thing.'

'It's a choice you can make,' Mark cajoled.

'You mean…?'

'Here, now. Call it research, if you like – a catalyst to move your life forward. You've told me how you feel you've reached a plateau, have been longing to ring the changes. If it helps to have an excuse, well, you've neglected your official duties this evening, and someone really should take you to task. Just what is your party's policy on corporal punishment?'

'We're all for it, but a soft liberal like you wouldn't dare,' she goaded.

'Look at me as the chief whip,' he said with deliberate irony, and without further delay grabbed Josephine around the waist and with little difficulty pulled her down over his knee. 'Nothing like a return to traditional values,' he continued, raising the sensible skirt to her waist. 'And just as I suspected, you have a perfect peach of a bottom,' he added admiringly.

Unsure whether the compliment or her predicament was making her blush, Josephine felt she should at least protest. 'Oh, please don't smack me too hard,' she whimpered.

'I can't smack you at all as things stand,' said Mark in exasperation. 'Lift your hips.'

Meekly she did so, allowing him to tug her tights and knickers into a tangle around her thighs.

'Wanton women aren't allowed to keep their tights on,' he explained. 'In fact, they shouldn't be wearing them at all; stockings are much more sensual and make a master's life so much easier.'

'But my bottom's bare,' she wailed.

'And overdue for a thorough spanking.' Mark punctuated the words with a series of crisp slaps to her smooth white buttocks, causing her to wriggle animatedly on his lap, a stinging smart quickly spreading across the exposed skin. Methodically he brought his palm ringing down, alternating from cheek to rapidly reddening cheek. Still squirming Josephine felt a deep heat radiate towards her loins while her struggle to escape Mark's strong grip had the pleasant side effect of rubbing her naked sex against his jeans.

A novice at having her bottom smacked she kicked out wildly until Mark draped his right leg over her calves to hold them. Likewise her flailing hands were efficiently pinned into the small of her back. Held firmly in place, Josephine's already burgeoning excitement was further heightened by this efficient form of restraint.

Mark paused, and emboldened by her enthusiastic response, slipped a finger between her legs to seek out her throbbing clitoris. She gasped in delight, and far from protesting she urged him on. 'More… oh, that's lovely… oh, I think I'm going to come.'

'You certainly are,' he said, pushing two fingers deep into her sex, and slapped her crimson cheeks several more times with his other hand as he pistoned his fingers in and out of her vagina and Josephine, her sexuality now fully awakened, shuddered to a spectacularly voluble orgasm.

Tumbling to the floor she sat, dishevelled and ecstatic, gazing up at him. Then, tugging at his belt, she drew Mark to a standing position and knelt submissively before him, and unbuttoned his jeans as she pressed her lips to the solid lump inside them.

Probably unique in leaving the conference with a new sense of purpose, Josephine at once set about making radical changes to her life. A week later, confident and determined, she left the London flat, unrecognisable in her eldest daughter's jeans and sweatshirt, and headed for the West End.

As luck would have it, she was the only customer in the cutting salon, an establishment which bore absolutely no resemblance to her customary hairdressers, that morning. She liked Michael the stylist immediately, and once she gleaned his knowledge of fashion to be infinitely more diverse and up to date than hers, decided to take him into her confidence, which was an inspired decision since he was instantly taken by her plans to accomplish a complete makeover.

'This is a step into uncharted territory for me,' she admitted. 'You be my guide and I've a much better chance of success.'

Enthusiastically Michael agreed. 'Josephine, I'd be honoured to help,' he replied.

'Oh dear, that sounds terribly formal – I think you'd better call me Jo,' she decided; yet another life-enhancing whim.

Since business was so quiet Michael opted to take an immediate half-day holiday and led an expedition around Soho and Convent Garden where, gossiping and giggling, taking frequent breaks at bars and cafés, the pair spent a pleasurable day inflicting major collateral damage to Henry's credit card.

Michael's sense of colour and style was impeccable, and effortlessly he sought out chic shops and new looks. Jo was having the best of times, but at last, sadly, it was time to say farewell, promising faithfully to meet Michael in a few weeks' time and update him on progress. For now Jo needed to get her booty home, bag up her old apparel for Oxfam, shower and change. Then to set in motion the next part of her plan, which would begin with a phone call to make a date for later that same day.

Even had Henry returned to their London home early the chances are the self-obsessed politico would not have recognised his wife. The Home Counties perm had gone first, replaced by a short boyish style of Michael's own devising. Jo's revised make-up regime was spare but effective, the scoop-necked top flattered her figure and a short skirt swirled about her sheer stockinged legs. En route to her date she heard a sharp intake of breath as a commuter behind her on the underground escalator looked up. Probably one of Henry's constituents, Jo thought naughtily.

'Josephine…' Mark struggled to speak as he ushered her into his flat. 'This is completely unexpected. Sorry, but for someone who makes a living from words, I'm stuck. You look gorgeous, dazzling… oh hell, I sound like a thesaurus.'

'You're not bad yourself,' said the politician's wife, 'but my name's now Jo, a simple abbreviation so it's not really cheating.'

'Okay,' he replied easily. 'The rest of your life starts here, Jo. Fine, that's understood. Tell me,' he continued with a meaningful look, 'what had you in mind for this evening?'

'You're the master,' she replied flirtatiously.

'So you said on the phone, but think about it; the submissive holds the power. Ultimately the choices are yours.'

'To which end I've brought something you may find useful.' Jo reached into her bag and handed him a worn leather riding crop. 'Very effective for equine discipline, but I hope you'll find an alternative use.'

'No problem.' He kissed her long and sensuously, hands roaming across her buttocks. They shared a bottle of wine and sat together talking, Jo amusing him with a detailed account of her hectic, watershed day. But eventually conversation dwindled and Mark took the initiative.

'Now,' he said, 'down to business.' Sensitive to her nervousness he was quick to reassure. 'We'll start slowly and gently,' he said, 'which means you lowering yourself across my knee, toes and fingers touching the floor, head down and bottom up.'

Jo went willingly across Mark's lap, and bit her lip as he carefully raised her skirt in time honoured fashion, thrilled at the feel of his warm hands lightly stroking her flawless globes. '*Voila*! The perfect spanking position,' he murmured. 'You're a natural, Jo.' He continued to caress her curves, unhurriedly applying his palms to the seat of her satin knickers. 'Gorgeous. It seems almost a shame to mark such perfection. But a leisurely warm-up and then you'll discover the full implications of your decision to come here tonight.' And then he concentrated on spanking the full rounded cheeks, delighted at the way they quivered at each impact, the target area perfectly framed by taut suspenders and the darker welts of her stocking tops.

Jo gasped and panted in response, her hips jerking and toes drumming lightly on the floor as the cumulative effect of several dozen crisp smacks began to take effect.

'Enough,' he said after about five minutes. 'Stand and hold your skirt up while I arrange the furniture – and no rubbing.'

Buttocks pink and a deep glow sending urgent messages to her pleasure zones Jo surreptitiously risked a discrete massage of her sensually throbbing rear. Big mistake; a stinging impact on the back of her right thigh made her regret it instantly. 'I said no rubbing,' repeated a stern voice, reinforcing the point with a similarly hard slap to her left leg.

'Yow!' Jo wailed, drumming her heels on the floor to ease the smart. Her eyes moistened and she pouted petulantly. 'That's not fair.'

'Who said anything about fair?' Mark responded evenly, surveying his handiwork as livid finger marks showed through the sheer nylon. 'Now do as you're told this time and kneel up here.' He pointed to a low stool in the centre of the room. Meekly she obeyed, and once in position she had to grip the edge of the seat to maintain her balance, acutely conscious of her prominently displayed bottom.

Mark lifted her chin and gazed firmly into her eyes. Desire coursed through her veins, her insides melted, her sex throbbed, and she knew she'd do anything he ordered without hesitation. Their lips touched briefly.

'The executioner's kiss,' he said, pulling up her skirt and deftly folding it over her hips. 'We don't want anything getting in the way,' he added purposefully, lowering her expensive underwear, and sliding a hand beneath her raised bottom he adroitly explored the wetness that betrayed the extent of her arousal. She moaned ecstatically as he petted her for several minutes, before removing his hand and picking up an object from the table nearby.

'What's that?' she asked, straining to peer over her shoulder.

Mark smiled. 'A simple old-fashioned strap, not rocket science but, believe me, very effective.'

Without further comment he skilfully employed the worn leather to burnish the surface of her taut globes, and within a couple of minutes the true measure of the innocent looking object become apparent as a searing heat started to spread through her nates. Now each successive slap was greeted by a cry as Jo wriggled her tortured, smouldering rear, urgently trying to assuage her discomfort. Clinging to the stool she craved a moment's respite and was soon begging him to transfer his attentions to her aching sex.

Eventually Mark abandoned the strap to massage her ravaged cheeks.

'Oh, yes, that's lovely but, please touch me lower down.'

'Hmm, I wouldn't usually allow a break so early in proceedings, but as you're something of a novitiate in these matters perhaps a little interlude might be appropriate,' he mused.

Taking a pot of cold cream he softly rubbed the soothing ointment into her stinging orbs, the feel of his hands on her sensitised skin sending fresh waves of pleasure to every inch of Jo's trembling body.

Lewdly she pushed back her ravaged bottom in

invitation. Kneeling still, she hung on desperately to the stool as he carefully parted her moist lips and slowly finger-fucked her to the very brink of coming.

'Go on, Mark, put your cock in,' she gasped crudely. 'Please, every inch, stretch me, force it all the way in.' The bluntness of her language astounded them both.

'Oh no, not yet, he teased. 'I like to put the waiting into wanting. Ritual and anticipation are essential to CP, as you must be properly taught. Now stand up and put your hands behind your head. After such disgustingly lascivious behaviour and shocking words I shall undoubtedly have to make sure the next part of your chastisement is a good deal more severe.'

She complied instantly, his tone warning her against antagonising him further, passively permitting him to remove her clothes until, in only stockings, high heels and a necklace of fine gemstones, she awaited her master's pleasure.

Purposefully he flexed the riding crop. 'A sophisticated choice, and potentially a harsh one,' he began. 'Fortunately, the beauty of the crop is its potential for subtlety as much as severity. In a moment I shall demonstrate.'

Lightly he ran his tongue over each of Jo's erect nipples. She closed her eyes, shivering at the intense pleasure, then opened them wide in astonishment as he adroitly flicked the tip of the crop across each breast, brushing the engorged teats in the process.

'You see?' He stood back, and from behind her Jo heard a soft swish as the crop cut through the air, and whimpered anxiously as the leather flap at the tip slapped the soft pale flesh of her inner thighs. 'Subtle or severe,' he repeated. 'I could work my way thus across every inch of your body; indeed, some day I plan to do just that, holding you suspended between pain and pleasure with no choice but to endure and enjoy. But not this evening. In future we'll extend the threshold of your endurance further than you'd believe possible, but for the present half a dozen strokes will suffice.

Leaving her, hands still on her head and trembling with anticipation, Mark wound the seat of the stool to its fullest height and topped it with a thickly padded cushion.

'Over,' he ordered brusquely, and almost in a trance Jo complied, fingertips touching the carpet on one side, toes the other, just the way, she recalled, her master liked things to be.

'Legs together, please,' Mark intoned, taking a step backwards.

The first stroke whistled through the air and Jo cried out as the full springy length of the crop wrapped a horizontal line of fire around her already soundly spanked contours. A second, then a third stroke followed, each one below the other, delivered with exploding precision, decorating her full bottom with angry weals.

Jo wailed loudly at each thwacking impact, partly in distress, partly exaltation; if cathartic change was what she wanted then it had certainly arrived, but could she possibly endure any more?

'Three more.' Mark seemed in no doubt. 'One here.' He let the crop's tip touch the sensitive crease between bottom and thighs. 'Another here,' he traced a line an inch above her stocking tops. 'And the last we'll keep as a surprise. Ready?'

'Ready.' Despite her confused emotions and pain-etched posterior Jo's voice was steady.

The fourth stroke was harder than its predecessors, jolting her forwards across the stool in shock and anguish, feet kicking, a sharp cry wrung from her lips.

The fifth, delivered exactly where promised, seemed to slice into her flesh and was pure agony to endure; a band of molten pain. Frantically she scissored her calves, convinced she couldn't possibly take any further lashes.

'Open your legs.' Inwardly despairing she nevertheless obeyed immediately, lest he add extra strokes.

To Jo's relief the final cut was gentler, a token blow across the centre of both cheeks. Tossing the crop aside Mark stepped forward, held Jo's writhing hips steady, and with a single thrust filled her to the hilt just as she had begged him to do moments earlier. It was simply the best sex she'd ever had, she thought, seconds before her first ever multiple orgasm overwhelmed her.

Several weeks later Mark and Jo were returning from a discrete night out at the cinema. Just before midnight he pulled up outside her London flat; it was not, they'd decided, prudent for him to be seen accompanying her in just yet. She'd filed for divorce from Sir Henry, it was true, but the proceedings had yet to be completed and the decree nisi granted.

As Mark reached across to open the car door Jo noticed a light in the flat. 'That's weird,' she said. 'I'm absolutely sure I switched that bedroom light out. I only ever leave the one in the hall on.'

Mark looked up, following the direction of her gaze. 'I don't wish to be alarmist,' he said, 'but I thought I saw a shadow of movement.'

The couple looked at each other. 'Burglars?' Jo gasped.

'An intruder of some sort,' he said. 'Better call the police.'

'No, hang on, it could conceivably just be Henry come to pick something up,' she cautioned, 'and he'd be furious if we made a false alarm call, especially now he has the shadow home office brief. I'll go and have a look first. And it's okay, I've got my mobile to call for help if I need to.'

'In which case I'm coming with you,' he said firmly.

The key turned smoothly and quietly in the lock, and the front door of the flat fortunately opened without a squeak. On tiptoe they moved cautiously and silently along the hall. The light in Jo's bedroom was unmistakably on, and as they approached small scuffling sounds of movement came from within.

'I think someone's coming out,' she whispered urgently.

'Quick, get on that side of the door, I'll try and grab them,' Mark hissed.

The two had barely time to conceal themselves before a small dark figure hurried out of the bedroom. Jo extended a leg, neatly tripping the figure, who fell headlong into Mark's grasp. A brief but vigorous struggle ensued, culminating in all three bodies tumbling back through the door and onto the bedroom floor.

Jo jumped up quickly and reached for the light switch, and Mark pinned the intruder's arms and wrenched back a ski mask to reveal, to their mutual shock, Tara, Sir Henry's allegedly accommodating research assistant.

'Tara, what the hell are you doing here?' shouted a furious Jo. 'Call the police, Mark.'

'No, please!' Tara's voice was shrill, almost frantic. 'Not the police! No, it'd ruin everything.'

'By which you mean your promising career, no doubt,' Jo spat.

'Well, yes, but even worse than that.'

'What's worse?' asked Jo suspiciously. 'I think you'd better do some pretty quick explaining.'

Tara tripped over her words in her haste to reply. 'Henry – sorry, Sir Henry persuaded me to do it,' she admitted shamefacedly. 'He said you were planning to divorce him and ruin him financially with the settlement.'

'Really?' mused Jo. 'Well, *when*, not if, the divorce goes through I get fifty percent of Henry's assets; quite fair for fifteen years of solid support and self-sacrifice on my part. If you were any sort of competent researcher you'd know he'll still remain a very wealthy man and comfortably off.'

Mark's instinct was sharper. 'So Henry was using you to dig up dirt on Jo to use as ammunition in the negotiations and reduce the size of the payout.'

'Yes,' Tara was on the verge of tears. 'He promised he could get me a researchers position on television, said he'd influence with the right people.'

'I doubt he has any beyond drinking with a few over-the-hill producers at his club,' Jo said dismissively, 'but be that as it may,' what exactly did your search yield to assist this sordid little task? Let's see what's in your bag.'

The black rucksack was duly tipped onto the floor, revealing nothing more than some solicitor's letters and a copy of a recent CP magazine. 'It was in your bedside drawer,' whispered Tara, unable to look Jo in the eye.

'That's right, bedtime reading,' Jo said coolly. 'So you

thought this magazine might provide evidence of certain interests I'd rather not share with three million unsophisticated Sunday tabloid readers, did you? Not very sisterly, is it?'

Tara hung her head and said nothing.

'I still think we should call the police,' growled Mark, not bothering to conceal his mounting outrage.

'No, that's all right, Mark, thanks,' Jo said calmly, currently very much mistress of her own domain, 'I can handle this situation quite well by myself. I think a little bit of instant retribution is just what this young lady needs.'

Tara looked even more frightened; her face paled alarmingly. 'What... what sort of retribution?'

'On the plus side,' Jo smiled without any discernible trace of humour, 'it doesn't involve the constabulary, either now or in the future. Shame, actually; I've always wanted to make use of the fact the chief constable really is a good friend of mine.

'But on the negative side, from your point of view, at least,' she continued purposefully, 'you are going to get a good bare-bottomed hiding.'

'What?' Tara gasped. 'No, you can't...'

'Can and will,' said Mark, relishing the prospect and his chance of a grandstand view. 'You've nothing to bargain with, Tara. Far better to take your medicine with some shred of dignity and honour.'

Jo sat on the bed. 'Mark, bring her over here, please,' she commanded.

Struggling, as Tara rapidly realised, was pointless. A slender size eight and five foot two she was no match for either of them, and soon found herself draped inelegantly across Jo's elegant lap. Mark held her wrists, and Jo pinned her legs with her calf. 'I said bare and I meant it,' she affirmed unrelentingly, and to her mortification Tara's black leggings were dragged down to divulge nothing more substantial than the slenderest of thongs bisecting two small but beautifully rounded globes.

'Right, I take it this is your first time?' Jo said sternly.

'Y-yes,' whimpered Tara, resigned to her fate.

'Good, well object all you want, the walls are thick enough.'

And without further preamble Jo set about reddening Tara's captive rump, and Mark observed appreciatively how easily she had slipped into a complete reversal of her usual role, and that she spanked hard and enthusiastically. Brow furrowed with pleasurable concentration, a distracted smile upon her lips, Jo methodically turned Tara's cute little bottom a shade close to vermilion. With systematic application she worked on both cheeks, sometimes cupping her palm to produce a sharp report upon impact with the full swell of quivering flesh. With plenty of practice on the receiving end of a thorough spanking, she knew just how to bring tears to a girl's eyes.

Tara protested, plaintively, tearfully, vehemently, but all to no avail. Only after nearly ten minutes did Jo allow her own stinging hand to rest upon twin peaches that blazed like an electric fire. Across her lap, dishevelled and humiliated, Tara was only too aware of the throbbing pain in her roasted rump but, unprepared for the surge of arousal stealthily spreading through her lower torso, clenching her muscles and surreptitiously rubbing her aching sex against Jo's stockinged thighs. Her tormentor, too practised a submissive to miss such telltale signs, eased Tara's evident distress and confusion by softly stroking her well-spanked bottom.

With a nod to Mark she bade him open a bedside cabinet drawer and pass her the small object it contained. Her soothing fingers strayed from cheek to cleft, teasing and petting the pouting lips barely concealed by the abbreviated thong. Tara's wails meantime had mutated to purrs, but her voice rose as she felt Jo ease the scrap of material to one side and spread the petal-like lips of her labia to open the treasure within.

Deftly she inserted the small vibrator Mark had passed her, pressing its quietly buzzing length into Tara's slick pink passage until all six inches were fully buried. Then, moving the thong back into place, Jo skilfully used it to hold the vibrator firmly in place and lift the girl's buttocks to greater prominence.

Once again, but this time leaving long intervals between each ringing slap, she recommenced the process of retribution. Once again Tara yelped and moaned, the delicious vibrations tingling the length of her pleasantly plugged quim, countered by the waves of burning discomfort spreading across her poor punished bottom.

'Now,' said Jo decisively, 'I think we'll find this an excellent method of obtaining the full and frank truth about the exact nature your relationship with my erstwhile husband. Start talking, Tara.'

Between mews and moans Tara told them what they needed to know, Mark jotting down notes in his rapid shorthand. The upshot of Jo's inquisition was, yes, Tara was ambitious; she wanted a career in politics and was prepared to cut corners if it sped up the timescale. She was not, she said indignantly, career obsessed enough to have screwed Sir Henry, though if he continued to believe he was in with a chance that was all well and good.

Not that Henry had been denying himself the pleasure of young female flesh, Tara revealed, and her climax eventually arrived, her petite form jerking animatedly across the lap of Sir Henry's erstwhile wife, and judging by her blissful expression, was worth the tribulation she endured to earn it. Lying limp as a rag doll over Jo's knee she apologised fulsomely for her delinquent behaviour, expressing a sincere wish to make amends.

'Fine,' said Jo, satisfied she'd gleaned enough information. 'So Tara, you've two choices, either get out of politics altogether or join our team – which is it to be?'

'Our team?' said Mark.

'Our team,' Jo responded confidently. 'Tara isn't the only one harbouring political ambitions, and with you two running my election campaign I think I've a good chance of entering parliament.'

Tara was pragmatic enough to realise she had little choice. Demur, and Jo was supremely well connected enough to make sure she'd never work in the Palace of Westminster again. Agree, and she could hitch her wagon to a rising star.

'Okay, I'm in,' she said briefly, a glint in her eye. 'But first let me finish that apology.' Sliding to the floor she started to work Jo's skirt up her trim thighs, revealing fine black stockings; worn partly in deference to Mark's preference and also because they made her feel assuredly sexy. Jo, now reverting to a passive demeanour, leaned back on her elbows and prepared to relish yet another new set of sensations. Teasing her legs wider apart, Tara hooked a thumb into an expensive pair of knickers and drew them, with a silky swish, down over Jo's high-heeled feet. Then, kneeling between the older woman's wantonly parted thighs she bent her mouth to her flooding sex and adroitly began to tongue her hardening clitoris.

Within minutes Jo was sprawled back across the bed, letting lose little yelps of delight and kneading her breasts, hard nipples clearly visible through the silk of her shirt. Kneeling up, Tara placed a hand under each of Jo's knees, lifting her legs and spreading them even further akimbo, the better to send her probing lips and darting tongue around Jo's vagina.

'Mark,' Jo said thickly, dimly aware her beau had temporarily turned voyeur.

'Yes?' he replied vaguely, apparently frozen to the spot, watching the two women cavort before him.

'I'm sure there's something you could do for Tara…'

Which is all the encouragement any red-blooded male would require. Kneeling behind Tara he disposed of the thong with a single tug and, seizing the vibrator between finger and thumb, pulled it from her hot, slippery pussy and replaced it with the tip of his cock. Jo saw Tara's eyes widen, and then the girl pushed back against him, forcing his pulsating rod deeper into her clenching grip. Impaled upon his rampant cock and nearing her second crisis she worked ever harder, plunging her tongue far into Jo's velvety quim, simultaneously sliding a finger in and out of her hitherto virgin bottom, and when the final three-way coalition occurred the three collapsed, spent and smiling, dishevelled but deeply satisfied, entwined on Jo's bed.

'Well, since we've broken the ice I guess you two had better stay the night,' said Jo, with commendable understatement. So they did.

And what happened afterwards? No, of course Jo didn't move in with Mark, though they were often together. She hadn't wrested back control of her life to surrender it immediately, however desirable a man he might be; and especially since her close relationship with Tara was continuing to develop in all sorts of ways.

Rather, she left Henry to entertain his constituency cronies at the house in the Shires and made the London flat her home. She sprung her delighted offspring from the horrors of a single sex boarding school and enrolled them at the local mixed comprehensive. She re-enlisted on the photographic degree and began to take freelance commissions, and an early speculative effort – skilfully realised with a motor drive and long lens – together with the suggestion that neither Henry nor his latest 'actress companion' would care to see prints in the public domain turned up trumps by ensuring his complete compliance, and an early uncontested and very generous divorce settlement.

New Jo, new future. Sounds like a political slogan doesn't it? Perhaps she'll use it now that she, aided by the dynamic young research and speechwriting team of Mark and Tara, is standing for parliament, on a liberal ticket.

Getting it Taped

A large office building, deep in the heart of the City of London, built to a grand scale, not great architecture but with enough marble and hardwood employed in its finish to overawe those entering the vast pillared expanse of its lobby. Just as its builder intended, back in the days when Britain still guiltlessly exploited the benefits of the Empire and our Royal Navy ensured capitalist endeavours went unhindered. When bowler hat and pinstripe were still everyday essentials, deference to one's superiors not just expected but demanded as of right, when to be 'something in the city' was a sure sign of personal and social success.

Today the managers of august financial institutions within the famous Square Mile are a different breed altogether; as likely to be female as male, suited by Armani, booted by Gucci, clutching MBA's and full of the dreary nonsense of mission statements and performance monitoring. Let's take a closer look at how they work...

'Okay, 5.15pm, no sign of either of them leaving the building, better check things are going to plan. Hang on a minute, woops, wrong camera. Ah, that's better, floor two, deputy MD's office. Turn up the sound, tighten the focus and... *voila*! Today's in-house entertainment...'

'I'm sure you know why I've asked you to stay behind, Claire.'

Silence.

'Well, do you?'

'Yes, Ms Morrison.'

'One might have thought your last traumatic visit to my office would have been enough to teach you a lesson, but it seems not.' The older woman paced the floor angrily as she spoke. 'Evidently a painful session with this,' she waved a thick plastic ruler in illustration of her point, 'wasn't sufficient to make my message clear.

'Since when I've caught you making personal phone calls on at least two occasions, have I not? Which no doubt explains why you were late typing up my notes from Wednesday's meeting. So, if you want to keep this job you're going to have to shape up. Either that, or ship out now. I've obviously been much too lenient thus far, but not this week, my girl, oh dear me no. This week I've something which is absolutely guaranteed to instil some discipline into your slovenly person.'

Eyes gleaming with barely suppressed excitement she reached behind the desk and produced a thin, whippy cane that bent to almost a full circle in her well-manicured hands. Releasing one end Ms Morrison allowed the rattan to swish though the air, the tip thwacking loudly against the padded seat of her chair. Claire turned pale, but said nothing.

'Right, you know the routine, into the middle of the room, feet slightly apart, bend over and touch your toes. Now!' Ms Morrison's voice was exultant.

Unseen by the older woman Claire discretely switched on the intercom as she passed the imposing desk, then upon reaching the centre of the palatial office she stopped as directed and hesitantly bowed forward to grasp her ankles. Her supple body easily achieved the awkward position, which for the benefit of watchers emphasised her slender waist and shapely legs, naturally blonde hair falling forward to obscure her pretty, even-featured face.

Imperiously Ms Morrison strode to the centre of the room and used the end of the cane to flick the girl's short tartan skirt up to her waist; with a derisive snort she attempted to suppress the pang of envy she felt on appraising the girl's small firm bottom; a dancer's figure, feminine but with a coltish, muscular strength.

'You can keep those skimpy knickers on, they won't offer any protection, but we'll have these out of the way,' Ms Morrison sneered, pulling the sheer tights down towards the tops of the girl's fashionable, knee-length boots.

A small moan of trepidation escaped her victim.

'Yes, you might well be nervous,' snarled her smartly suited superior, a hint of cruel satisfaction in her voice. 'Keep still, you're getting six. Stand up, move your hands or make too much noise and I shall take great pleasure in starting all over again. And don't forget, girl, you agreed to this rather than be dismissed.'

Standing back she flexed the cane once more before slicing the air with a couple of practice strokes that made the unfortunate Claire wince. There were no further preliminaries, no lecture, no chance to repent sins real or invented. With a look of steely determination Ms Morrison measured her distance, lifted the bamboo high and rapidly delivered the promised half a dozen strokes in quick succession.

Claire barely had to time to experience the first impact before a second blazed a searing line of fire across her hindquarters. Ms Morrison was right; the skimpy knickers afforded little protection and her posterior was soon patterned with livid red stripes. Each scalding blow was applied to the shivering globes with the full force her tormentor could muster. At the third stroke she cried out, by the sixth poor Claire was rocking back on her heels, buttocks clenching, cheeks aflame, sobbing with pain and distress.

'Stand up,' ordered her punisher curtly, taking a step back to survey her handiwork. Six livid red almost horizontal wheals had scored the girl's tender buttocks. The ends of two or three strokes overlapping slightly to produce ugly blue bruises which would take hours to stop throbbing and days to fade. Displaying laudable fortitude under the circumstances, the girl slowly and uncomfortably straightened, hands desperately rubbing her burning bottom in a futile bid to soothe the soreness.

Then the office door flew open dramatically and in strode a tall, fair-haired young man, older than the softly weeping blonde, a little younger than her boss.

'Michael!' Ms Morrison shrieked, aghast.

'I don't believe it!' he exclaimed, genuinely shocked by the scene before him. 'I came as soon as you gave the signal, Claire, but it seems I'm too late.' Striding to her side Michael put a comforting arm around the girl's shoulders, discreetly lowering his gaze to look in horror at the livid purple lines criss-crossing her pert buttocks.

'Well, this certainly substantiates everything you told me, I can see now you weren't exaggerating.' He passed her a large handkerchief. I can't believe such a thing

could take place in this day and age and in this office.'
He shook his head in amazement. 'But I'm afraid the
evidence is quite beyond doubt.

'Don't let me detain you further, Claire,' he added
gently. 'You've obviously been through enough for one
day. Go home, but don't worry, I won't let this matter
drop; it's high time Ms Morrison and I had a serious
discussion about this incident, the like of which, you have
my word, will not be permitted to ever occur again.'

'Thu-thank you,' Claire managed between sobs, drying
her eyes, and then with considerable dignity she walked
stiffly from the room, leaving the outraged middle
manager to confront the eponymous Ms Morrison.

Seizing the moment, Michael snatched the cane from
her grasp as she remained rooted to the spot, transfixed
with shock and surprise. 'So this is your idea of modern
management, is it? What the hell do you think you're
doing, Sally, running some sort of personal crusade to
return to Victorian values? God knows what the boss
will think of this.'

A look of fear crossed Sally's face. 'You wouldn't let
on?' she said desperately. 'I mean, we're equals, you
can't go telling tales.'

'Stopping you beating your temp is hardly telling tales,'
Michael responded, his voice threatening. 'Bloody hell,
woman, what happened to your sense of perspective? I
knew you were ambitious right from the start, and it's
been obvious to everyone for some time that you were
taking the job far too seriously, working all hours, no
social life; but this?' He sounded incredulous.

'It – it's not easy being the only woman at this level of
management,' Sally bumbled defensively, 'Besides, the

girl was sloppy.'

'Oh please, spare me the excuses,' Michael replied levelly. 'How dare you abuse your position to take your frustrations out on the most junior staff?'

Sally continued to try and fight her corner, but with little success.

'When you were appointed a few months back,' Michael cut in, 'I was introduced to an attractive, intelligent, highly capable professional who, initially, it was a pleasure and privilege to work with. Since when it's no secret you broke up with a longstanding partner because of the hours you put in here. Colleagues were ready to be sympathetic if you'd let them, but instead you just buried yourself in the job. People who cared, who wanted to help – including me, you may recall – got the rough edge of your tongue and eventually gave up. Junior staff live in terror of your moods, peers avoid you because you've become a humourless obsessive. Now you've lost the plot completely.'

Sally's shoulders slumped, for a moment she sank her head into her hands then, decisively, shook back her dark hair and fixed Michael with a candid gaze. 'I guess there's not much I can disagree with in your assessment,' she began dejectedly. 'Looking back, I suppose I thought I had to prove myself, go it alone, be seen to be independent and decisive. But instead of appearing strong and capable I've become isolated and aloof, caught in a self-perpetuating circle, the less I was liked the worse I behaved. Now you're off to the boss and I've blown my chance. The other female staff won't care; why should they offer me support? All those years studying, working at forging a successful career in international finance wasted, my job and my life both down the drain.'

There followed a long silence, finally broken by Michael.

'A possible scenario, but the future doesn't have to be like that,' he said carefully. 'In fact, I'm still prepared to help, if you want me to.'

With the look of a drowning woman grasping at a straw Sally's reply was unhesitating. 'Oh, I do, I do!'

Michael fixed her with an unblinking stare, and after a long tense silence he spoke. 'I believe you, though others might not, but just because I'm prepared to show some compassion for your self-inflicted plight doesn't mean you should escape the consequences of your actions. To ensure a complete change of attitude you'll need a change of heart. It's not your staff who deserve to be punished, Sally, it's you, and the choice I'm offering is difficult but very simple.

'Accept the same punishment as you gave your PA,' he continued, 'and the incident is forgotten, we can move on. I'll smooth things over with Claire and give you any assistance I can to get you back on track. Refuse, and I'll have no hesitation in shopping you to the board.'

For a moment Sally looked aghast. 'Y-you mean, cane me?' she finally whispered.

'Certainly,' Michael confirmed. 'You'd no compunction about dishing it out.'

'But, but,' she hesitated, her brain in turmoil, surely there must be another way? An impatient look on Michael's face told her time was running short, she was backed into a corner, there was no alternative, accepting his ultimatum was her only chance. 'But, you're right,' she agreed heavily. 'I've no other option... I agree to your terms.'

'Good,' Michael said briskly. 'In which case there's no time like the present. However, since you're a grown woman, not some slip of a girl, I'm going to reinforce the lesson and instil some humility by spanking you first. Come here.' Michael sat on a straight-backed chair, his steely-grey eyes drawing her hypnotically towards him. 'Take off your jacket.'

She did so, revealing prominent breasts beneath her blouse.

'Now lift your skirt.'

Reluctantly, Sally hoisted up the conservative, knee-length black skirt to reveal dark stockings, suspenders and high-cut silk knickers; a far more exotic taste in underwear than Michael would ever have expected.

'Very nice,' he said dryly, tipping her over his lap.

'Am I in time Joe? What've I missed?'

'Yes you are, and not a lot. So far things have panned out pretty much as you predicted. Michael read the riot act and threatened to tell the boss, unless...'

'She accepts his punishment?'

'Exactly, you know for a resting actress – nay, a consummate song and dance entertainer – you're no mean psychologist when it comes to sizing people up.'

'Thanks for the compliment, kind sir; for an apprentice actor you make a fine security guard. Fortunately for you I love a man in uniform.' Claire smiled wickedly before continuing. 'However, I put my accurate predictions of people's likely reactions down to good old fashioned feminine intuition. I can recognise a dominant man when I see one, and you're proof positive enough of that, Joe.'

'True,' he agreed amiably. 'But back to the plot, allow me to continue to update the story so far. Sally initially tried to bluff it out but eventually realised the situation was hopeless. Strangely, she almost looks relieved.'

'Well, he is quite a dish…'

'She's rather gorgeous too.'

'Mm, methinks that's male speak for "certainly not last in the queue when they doled out the boobs". I wonder if she's got a bum to match?'

'Meow! Could that be a green tinge to your skin, perchance? Anyway, hush or we'll never find out. Sit down and watch.'

'Sit down? No thank you.'

'Oops, sorry I forgot, thoughtless of me since I've seen you take a thrashing on screen which made my eyes water just watching. All right, tell you what, lean on the desk in front of the monitor, you can still watch events unfold from there and I'll rub some cold cream into those stripes.'

'Mmm, you're too kind, sir, but please be careful when touching my poor little bum…'

Sally soon discovered to her cost the pointlessness of trying to escape Michael's muscular grasp. Her attempts to wriggle free from his lap and avoid the steady onslaught of slaps that stung her rearmost curves like a patch of nettles had so far only resulted in a further series of indignities.

First Michael pinned her flailing hands firmly behind her back. Then he used his leg to trap her shapely, nylon-clad legs and stop them from kicking the air. Further humiliation followed as he hiked her knickers up into the deep valley between her buttocks and exposed even more taut, pale flesh to be reddened by his relentless right hand.

Suddenly the fight went out of her and as she relaxed he released her pinioned limbs and began to caress her beleaguered behind, now radiating a fierce heat all of its own. As his fingers softly traced the sore contours Sally felt a warmth overwhelm the pain in her tender bottom, spread slowly through her pelvic region and stimulate her sex with urgent desire. With a groan of yearning she languidly surrendered to the thrilling, long repressed sensation of sexual desire.

'I do rather think Ms Morrison is beginning to enjoy the experience of having her gorgeous rear tanned,' Joe commented laconically.

'Um, I know how she feels,' Claire sighed dreamily as her own bottom was gently massaged. 'The young master certainly seems to know what he's about, and if I'm not mistaken Sally has reached the point where pain and pleasure become blurred. Right now she'll be aching for something to fill that void inside, secretly hoping he'll slide a hand between her thighs and pay some attention to that sadly neglected pussy.'

'Like this, you mean?' murmured Joe, skilfully slipping two cream-slicked fingers into her sopping sex while a third gently teased her engorged clitoris.'

Claire clenched her thighs tightly together and sighed deeply in mute reply.

Just as a desperately needed climax built within Sally, so she was rudely decanted from Michael's lap to kneel confused, dishevelled and frustrated on the carpet before him, her appearance in stark contrast to the ice-maiden of some fifteen minutes previously. Several buttons on her creased white blouse were undone, revealing a generous expanse of cleavage, heaving from her exertions. Contrary to its advertised claims, the expensive non-smudge lipstick had failed its consumer test and her eye make-up had run with tears. Her carefully styled hair looked windswept and as she turned she was appalled to observe her crimsoned bottom, liberally decorated with the overlapping handprints of the man towering resolutely above her.

'Let's not forget the primary purpose of this encounter, Ms Morrison,' Michael continued sternly, very much in command of the situation. 'You are here to be punished. This, as I indicted at the start, was merely a warm-up to get you in a receptive state of mind and body. You'll find the cane considerably more severe.'

In order to emphasise the total power he enjoyed over her, Michael paused for theatrical effect, conscious his last statement would finally dash any slim hopes of mercy Sally may have entertained. Extending a hand he hauled her inelegantly to her feet.

'Skirt and knickers right off, I don't want anything in the way of what I fully intend to be an exemplary beating of your completely unprotected bare buttocks. Get right over the desk, grasp the far edge with both hands, knees together, legs straight and push that bottom right out,' he ordered brusquely.

Unaccustomed to being spoken to in such authoritarian

terms, Sally complied robotically. No longer in control of events, no decisions to make, she'd merely to obey his will. Curiously she felt a strange sense of freedom, almost as if a weight had been lifted from her shoulders. Discarding her lower garments as instructed she stretched penitently across the polished wooden top, and felt the polished wood press hard against her engorged nipples, cool against her flat stomach, aware of her vulnerability, of her dark curly pubic hair failing to conceal her damp sex from Michael's appreciative view.

'Gorgeous bum, you have to admit,' Claire commented languorously as she avidly watched the drama unfold. Joe was deftly creating waves of pleasure between her parted legs; two fingers busy in her fanny, his thumb penetrating her anus, his other hand toying with two prominently erect nipples, the overall effect sending further jolts of desire through her willowy frame.

'Not a patch on your cute little butt,' replied her beau chivalrously. 'But in truth, the hitherto loathsome Ms Morrison is possessed of a fine pair of pins.'

'Ah, the seductive lure of the mature woman, or are you just a sucker for stockings and suspenders?' giggled Claire. 'Tell you what; I'll wear some on our day off tomorrow, with no knickers. How about that?'

The mere thought hardened Joe's growing erection still further. 'Now that's finesse,' he said admiringly as Michael lay a second cane stroke across the centre of Sally's pert posterior. 'None of the hard and fast brutality the mare used on you.' He crouched to run his tongue delicately across each of the cane marks still vividly etched across Claire's bottom.

'Don't remind me,' she groaned, squirming ecstatically as he kissed her glistening cleft, deftly moving to seek out her erect clitoris, 'my bum's going to be marked for days. I reckon I'll be eating standing up all weekend.'

'Not the only thing you'll be doing standing up…' Joe whispered suggestively.

'Patience, young man, they're not finished yet,' giggled Claire, reaching back to grasp his rock hard erection. 'Don't get so carried away with lust you forget what this little game was all about in the first place. Do you reckon our idea's worked?'

'Can't see it going wrong; in return for copies of this tape I reckon our two ambitious, upwardly mobile deputy MD's will be pleased to shell out more than enough to top up our grants until we take the final exams next summer – and even pay for a dirty weekend away into the bargain.'

Knuckles white from gripping the desk edge so tightly, brow furrowed and beaded with perspiration, Sally lay across the polished mahogany struggling to regain her composure, her posterior scored with six fiery stripes, each flashing a painful message to every nerve-ending in her body. It took an interval of several minutes before her toes at last stopped drumming on the carpet and her ragged breathing returned to something approaching normal.

'You may get up now.'

'Michael…' Sally's voice was weak, but she continued, as surprised as he by what she had to say, '…you gave me six strokes, the same number as Claire. But I abused my authority and trust; I deserve two more.'

113

Did she really say that? Inviting further chastisement when every inch of her soundly beaten bottom was sore to even the most tentative touch.

'She wants more,' said Joe incredulously as they watched from the security office. 'I don't understand it.'

'I do,' whispered Claire.

'Very well,' Michael's tone was solicitous. For a moment time seemed to stand still, then a familiar whistling sound cut the air. Somehow Sally forced up her haunches, arching her body to meet the molten band of hurt that slashed down cruelly – once, twice, biting sharply into the crease between her bottom and thighs. Eyes blurred with tears but somehow managing a triumphant smile, she turned to face the tall man.

'There's one more thing you can do for me,' she breathed seductively, reaching for his zip. 'After taking that penance with such fortitude I think I've earned an executive bonus.'

Michael's strong hands lifted her effortlessly. Sally gasped as her ravaged flesh met the desk's unrelenting surface, then again as the full throbbing length of his cock entered and filled her to the hilt with a single lunge. Tugging at her blouse he wrenched it open, taking each nipple in turn into his mouth through the lace of her bra. Clutching his broad shoulders Sally urgently pushed her hips forward to meet and absorb each deeply penetrating thrust, sinking her teeth into his neck, urgently abandoning herself to everything but a lust-fuelled desire for sexual fulfilment.

'My turn now,' moaned Claire, naked from waist to toes. 'I want to be fucked too.' Obediently Joe held her hips and delivered a command performance, easing his erection into her passion-swollen sex from behind. 'Oh, it's so big,' she gasped in delight, forced up onto tiptoe as she struggled to accommodate him. 'I'm only small… I may not be able to take it all.' But she did. Twice.

Once from the rear, then again lingeringly on the office floor, Joe carefully pushing her knees up to her breasts to keep her ruthlessly beaten bottom from chafing on the carpet; a consideration for which she was doubly grateful since it increased the depth of his entry, filling her completely and ensuring another shattering climax.

Afterwards, as they lay together on the plush carpet in satiated contentment, Sally noticed the little red light flashing on the wall-mounted camera. 'Oh no, we're being filmed!' she gasped.

Michael didn't even bother to stop kissing her exquisite breasts. 'Watched possibly, recorded no,' he stated quietly. 'We'd a report of some computer discs being stolen, so I took the tapes out of the security machine at lunchtime to check them.' His tongue continued on down…

Well, who's to say it never happened?

Home Service

Already five minutes late for his first appointment of a busy spring morning, James quickly shoved two hours' worth of coins into the parking meter, buzzed the intercom and took the stairs to the third floor of the student halls two at a time.

A slim female answered his discrete knock at an anonymous door, apparently in her late teens. James made a quick visual appraisal of his client: long fair hair lightened by streaks of silver and blond, some strands plaited with bright ethnic beads, a symmetrically pretty face, turned up nose and young enough to be his daughter. Umm, could be a problem, he thought before flashing a practised smile.

'Hello, I'm James.'

'Hi, I'm Kerry. Come in.'

She waved him into an extremely compact beds, decorated with posters of contemporary pop icons, all totally unfamiliar to him. Whatever happened, James wondered briefly, to Pink Floyd?

'Kerry, before we begin,' he started, 'please don't think me rude, but could I confirm your age?'

She smiled ruefully. 'No offence taken, I knew I should have worn make-up. Nineteen, two weeks ago. I could show you my birth certificate?'

'No, thanks,' James held up his hands in mock surrender. 'That's fine; we might as well start by trusting each other. Now, what did you have in mind?'

She paused, coloured slightly, and took a deep breath. 'I've never done anything like this before,' she confessed.

Ever patient, James smiled encouragingly, waiting for her to continue in her own good time.

'You see, I've been reading these magazines,' Kerry, sitting cross-legged on the single bed, gestured to a small pile of top-shelf CP publications in one corner. 'Amazing how your literary horizons expand when you leave home.' She leant forward, clasping her knees to her chest, her expression earnest and sincere.

'Well, the idea of being punished turns me on, at least in theory. To tell the truth, I'm not yet very sexually experienced. Despite what you may hear about students it's not all drunken parties; these days most of us are working too earnestly, trying to get grades good enough to secure a well paid job that will pay off our student loans.

'I mean,' she continued hastily, 'I'm not a blushing virgin or anything, but before introducing any sort of CP into a relationship I'd like to try it in safer circumstances first.'

James nodded. Her candour was engaging; he couldn't imagine a male being so frank.

'So you've booked me to provide a taster session. A test run, with no emotional complications. At the risk of sounding patronising, that's a very mature approach.'

'Oh, thank you for saying so,' Kerry said, favouring him with a beaming grin. 'That's it, exactly. Oh, I am glad you understand. I thought if you could, you know, perhaps spank me first, not too hard, then if I enjoyed it we might progress a bit further – perhaps try, you know, some sort of implement?'

'Fine by me,' James looked around. 'Although there's hardly room to swing the proverbial cat in here, I'm sure we'll manage,' he added reassuringly then, abruptly changing tone, sternly issued a pre-emptory command. 'Come here, Kerry. At once girl, hurry up.'

Hands clasped before her, studiously avoiding eye contact, she stood and shuffled slowly towards him. 'Yes sir?' she whispered.

A natural, thought James. A good few inches shorter than him she wore a sleeveless T-shirt, tucked into faded baggy jeans, tightly cinched around a waif-like waist by a webbing belt. Surely not short of admirers, but would someone her own age have the experience and confidence to take her in hand? James doubted it.

'Really, this is quite deplorably irresponsible of you,' he said. 'A well brought up girl, inviting strangers to your room. It's high time you were disciplined, my girl.'

She stood quietly; eyes focused into the middle distance as James reached forward, loosened her belt and slid the jeans down over her hips to revealed a pair of snug white cotton knickers.

'Naughty girls are never, ever punished over clothes,' he continued sonorously, and for want of much choice sat on the single bed, pulling Kerry, unprotesting, across his lap.

'This is where your fantasies become reality, young lady. Time for this pretty little bottom to receive a thorough spanking.' Kerry made no reply, but James felt a tremor run through her body as she shifted, attempting to make the unfamiliar position more comfortable, her toes barely touching the floor, her weight light across his knees.

Smoothing the creases from her underwear his palm unhurriedly explored the flawless skin of her unmarked posterior. Deliberately letting the tension build he softly caressed the soft yielding globes for some minutes, before beginning to spank the proffered cheeks. Easy does it, no hurry.

To start with James concentrated his efforts on the pale crown of each springy buttock, delighting in the way the firm flesh bounced and rippled beneath his hand. Her upper body supported by the bed, hands cupping her chin, Kerry responded to each ringing slap with tiny exhalations, gasps and groans. Gradually her bottom cheeks turned pink, she squirmed on his lap and the gasps gave way to little cries that mingled anguish and excitement.

He continued, gradually increasing the area of flesh to feel the sting of contact with his practised palm, until Kerry's entire bottom had received similar treatment and was uniformly red and warm to the touch.

'How does that feel?' he asked at last.

'Oooh, it stings, my bottom feels hot all over,' she said uncertainly.

'Does it hurt?'

'Yes, but it's a nice hurt.'

James ran his fingers across the tops of her thighs, traced the line of her perineum beneath the now damp cotton, and felt Kerry press her hips down onto his legs in mute reply. 'Right,' since his palm had begun to smart it was evidently time for a break in proceedings, 'stand up and look in the mirror.' Kerry scrambled to her feet and, twisting round to peer over her shoulder, surveyed his handiwork. Her agitated wriggling had worked her knickers into the cleft of her buttocks, the white material accentuating her burning red backside.

'Ooh, you cruel man, my poor little bum's so sore,' she pouted. 'Can I rub it, please?'

'As it's the first time, I think I can permit that,' he consented, flattered that she'd thought to seek his assent. Kerry's left hand urgently began massaging her seared cheeks, but her right sneaked inside the front of her knickers, fingers anxious to ease a quite different sort of ache.

This was enough to raise more than James' eyebrows. 'What do you think you're doing?' he asked with convincing outrage. 'That spanking's obviously had no effect at all. I shall undoubtedly have to be more severe.'

'Oh sir, what will you do now?' she wailed.

No doubt about it, she wanted to continue...

'Take your jeans off completely,' he ordered. 'Put that chair in front of the mirror and kneel on it, hands on your head. It's high time you had a dose of the strap.'

While Kerry scurried to obey James rummaged in his holdall for a two-tailed tawse; an old favourite, well worn by years of application to delinquent behinds. 'You'll take six,' he informed her firmly, 'on the bare.'

'Oh sir, no sir,' gasped Kerry, making no attempt to move.

Wearing only the singlet and a pair of short white socks she assumed an authentically sulky expression, eyes warily watching his reflected image as he drew her knickers down to her knees.

Measuring his distance he drew back his arm; Kerry tensed and screwed her eyes tight shut. For a moment, time stopped.

Thwack!

Six methodical strokes covered the crown of her buttocks; six ever-louder cries escaped Kerry's lips. Her feet kicked the air, fingers clutched at her hair, pert posterior danced and twisted to the tawse's tune.

As the final stroke kissed her firm young flesh she cried out, half in pain, half in triumph, stretched towards the ceiling then slumped forward, grasping the back of the chair for support. A hand slid slyly back between her thighs. Moments passed. James waited tolerantly, allowing Kerry time to regained her composure.

'Wow, that was amazing!' she enthused wearily. 'I wasn't expecting an orgasm as well – not the first time. You really are good at your job.' She gingerly pulled her panties up over her sore bottom. 'I think we've answered a few questions,' she continued huskily. 'Thank you, James.'

'Thank you,' he replied, and meant it.

'How much do I owe you?' she asked, reaching a little shakily for her bag.

'It's usually eighty pounds a session, but student grants seem to have disappeared since my day, so let's call it a round sixty.'

'Generous, too.' That heartstopping smile again, and then she kissed him warmly on the cheek. Sometimes professional detachment was hard to maintain. It was time to go.

Two minutes later James was back in the van heading towards the West End, wryly reflecting that there were worse ways to earn a living.

Ironically, it was his wife Mona who had started it. They'd been watching a television documentary about the female clients of Australian male prostitutes; guys who visited their clients at home, in hotels, even clandestinely at work. According to Mona's view of things James had much in common with the show's star; both were carpenters, assiduous, highly-skilled craftsmen who produced beautiful woodwork but found it hard to make ends meet in a world geared to mass production.

'So what?' he asked, incredulous at the turn the conversation appeared to be taking. 'You think I should give up woodwork and become some sort of a gigolo?'

'I don't think I could bear you selling your body to other women,' Mona said. 'Not that there wouldn't be plenty of takers,' she added, shooting him an appreciative glance. 'But unarguably you have got other talents.' She made a show of rubbing her glowing backside, a reminder of spontaneous fun and games earlier in the evening, to emphasise the point.

'Plus you're a good communicator, thankfully not vain, in great shape, and take a pride in everything you do.' Mona paused from the list to draw breath, and then delivered the clinching point. 'And an expert at warming a girl's bum.'

James laughed. 'Thanks for the testimonial, I'm sure they'd be impressed at the job centre.'

'No, I'm serious.' Mona developed her argument, 'Look at all these CP books and magazines that have blossomed over the last few years. Someone must be reading them, and I'll bet a lot are independent, financially secure women who'd welcome a real-life session with no strings attached.'

It may have seemed a joke at the time but here, a year later, James was employed virtually full-time smacking willingly presented female bottoms, a job the majority of red-blooded males in Britain would have done for free, let alone the extremely good living he was currently making.

Initially he had not shared his wife's confidence and needed a lot of persuasion. But after only a few weeks discrete, carefully worded ads in upmarket specialist publications had produced a steady stream of requests to be checked and vetted by Mona. It was she who effectively managed the new enterprise, set the prices, vetted the clients and arranged the schedule. James had become a professional dominant, but Mona remained in charge.

There were three visits on the computer printout today. One down, two to go. The next call was a regular customer, every fourth week for the last five months, repeat business from a satisfied client and always at the same venue. James parked the van beneath an imposing tower block, changed into a smart suit from the costume wardrobe in the back and, already familiar with the building's door security codes and the routine expected of him, made his way discretely and unobserved to an office on the top floor.

He'd scarcely time to seat himself behind the imposing yet curiously bare desk, pour a glass of mineral water and admire the view across miles of urban landscape, before there came a knock on the door.

'Enter,' his voice had now assumed an imperious quality.

A poised, elegant woman in her thirties did so. 'You sent for me, sir?'

'Yes, take a seat please, Ms Jones.'

She sat on the only available chair, knees together and hands twisting nervously in her lap. 'Is there a problem?'

'Most definitely,' James said sombrely. He paused to glare at her before continuing in a cold authoritative tone. 'I've been looking through this month's figures, where I regret to observe there's been no improvement.'

The silence was deafening.

'I'm sorry,' Ms Jones said at last, humbly.

'Unfortunately sorry doesn't cut it.' James raised his voice. 'Last time we met I believe I made it crystal clear what would happen if you failed to better your performance.'

'Oh no.' Trepidation was written all over her blushing face, the beautifully made-up eyes brimmed with tears, pearl-white teeth nibbled anxiously at a crimson lip.

'Oh yes, such idleness merits far more serious treatment than a mere spanking or the strap. Your insolent, lazy bottom has clearly absorbed nothing from my punishments thus far, so this time it's the cane for you, young woman. And I can promise you'll howl at every single stroke. Prepare yourself at once, in precisely one minute from now I want you bare bottomed across my desk.'

Wretchedly, she obeyed. First the well-cut linen jacket was discarded onto the chair. Hastily she undid the perfectly tailored skirt, wriggling the material over trim hips then elegantly stepping out of it without catching her black high heels.

Scarlet with shame and humiliation she looked

hopefully at James, mutely pleading for mercy. 'I said bare bottomed,' he insisted icily, pointedly ignoring the appeal implicit in her wide green eyes. 'You have fifteen seconds before earning additional strokes, which I shall be only too pleased to deliver hard across your pampered arse.'

Stung by the deliberate cruelty explicit in his choice of words a tear meandered down Ms Jones' cheek as she slid her knickers down shapely, stockinged legs. Shakily she walked to the desk, bent fully across the cold polished surface and silently grasped the other side.

'Thank you,' James said crisply, and adjusted her pose to his preferment. 'Stomach flat on the desk, push your buttocks out as far as you can, legs straight and just a fraction apart. Try not to tense up too much, Ms Jones. Ah, splendid.'

And a splendid sight it certainly was. What a pity client confidentiality didn't permit him the chance to immortalise the scene with a photograph. The high heels tightened her calves and thighs, rendering the beautifully rounded buttocks, bordered by black suspenders and the welts of her sheer stockings, all the more prominent and inviting.

'And what happens now?' he demanded.

'You punish me.' Her voice quavered enticingly.

'Punish you, what?!' he barked.

'Punish me please, sir?' she offered.

'Better, but this is rather more than a mere punishment, is it not?'

'Yes sir, it's the punishment I richly deserve, sir.'

'And…?'

'And the punishment I richly deserve…' her voice

125

faded as she struggled to finish the dreadful phrase, 'is a thrashing with the cane on my wicked bare bottom, sir.' The final words tumbled out in a rush, ending in sob of helplessness and resignation.

James stepped back, lightly resting the cane on the crown of her buttocks. Ms Jones whimpered at the contact. James stood motionless, until the tension became unbearable and Ms Jones was shamefully reduced to pleading for him to begin.

'Please…' she ventured desperately. 'Please cane me now.'

James uncompromisingly brought the bamboo flashing down. At the first stroke she yelped. The second stripe, an inch lower, wrenched a moan from her lips as she squirmed and struggled to maintain her grip on the desk's edge.

Strokes three and four fell exactly parallel, one above, one below the first pair. Her feet stamped the floor, she squealed, oblivious to the possibility of others in the building hearing her distress, savouring the humiliation of a senior manager who took herself so seriously, grinding her hips onto the polished surface of the desk and frantically grasping the far edge, trying to stay in position and avoid the terrifying possibility of penalty strokes.

James allowed an interval and felt Ms Jones' taut body relax as he ran a palm cross the livid tracks etched into her soft skin. He traced the cleft between her buttocks, slithered his fingers over her seeping sex, and stroked the insides of her thighs. 'Bad girl,' he admonished gently.

Ms Jones raised her head, expensively coifed hair now

tousled and awry.

'Look,' he thrust the evidence of her arousal before her, and obediently she licked his fingers, slowly, seductively sucking each one.

'Back down,' he ordered curtly, and with a moan of despair she braced herself for the concluding strokes. 'Pull yourself right up onto the desk.'

Puzzlement crossed her face; this wasn't part of the usual ritual.

A line of fire seared the backs of her thighs. 'That one doesn't count, now do as you're told,' he snapped viciously.

Hurriedly she slid across the desk's shiny surface.

'Better.' James stood at her feet, raised the slender wand to shoulder height and brought it streaking down. Ms Jones jerked violently as a livid welt appeared, running up her buttock to the right of her shadowy cleft.

Her wail of surprise was cut short by the *thwip*! of a second stroke, bisecting the left cheek in a similar manner and, like the former, agonisingly cutting across each of the four previous stripes. Hips bucking wildly she howled in anguish, her hands flying back to rub her pain-filled, crimson-lined posterior.

James moved smoothly to a desk drawer, where he knew from previous visits she'd circumspectly hidden a vibrator of impressive dimensions, and handed it to Ms Jones. 'Let me know if you want to book the same time next month,' he said simply, moving towards the office door.

On her back, on her desk, Ms Jones nodded distractedly, already absorbed in bringing events to a climax, sliding the gently humming plastic deep inside her, an abundance of feminine juices easing its passage.

No one in the firm dared confront her power, and lovers seemed always too intimidated by her wealth and success to take her in hand as she needed to satisfy the craving deep within, so, as usual, she had to take on the responsibility herself.

Quietly James closed the door behind him. *Ms E Jones – Managing Director* stated the gold embossed nameplate on the outer side.

The last call was in a northern suburb. At length, after much cursing of slothful traffic and with a silent prayer of thanks to the A-Z's assiduous publishers, James walked up the front path of a nondescript semi-detached house, just as an attractive Asian woman opened the door.

'Hello, you must be James,' she welcomed. 'Do come in, I've been looking out for you.' Thankfully the interior decor was an improvement on the mundane outside; stripped and polished floors, warm terracotta colours, typical nineteen-nineties middle class taste with a dash of style where Asia and the old world met in the form of rugs, fabrics and ornaments; hinting at a country his host probably knew only from her parent's stories and occasional extended holidays.

Surinder had dark expressive eyes, waist-length raven-black hair, and a slight yet curvaceous figure that, James thought, perfectly complimented the warmth of her open, sensuous smile.

'Nice to meet you, Surinder.' They shook hands formally.

'You too, James, thanks for journeying so far out into the bush,' she joked, a mischievous glint in her eye.

'No problem, did you have anything special in mind?' he enquired discretely.

'I certainly do.' The reply was confident and assured. 'I'm hoping we'll benefit from your skills as a teacher. Your manager was most confident you'd be able to help.'

'We?'

'This is Jamal.' She introduced a tall good-looking man who stood hitherto unnoticed by James, diffident in a corner of the front room. 'He's a little embarrassed by all this.

'You see,' Surinder continued, 'traditionally Asian women are not supposed to be so up front about their desires and, although we were both born and educated here absorbing western attitudes and values, he's still a little old fashioned. In everything else – our jobs, our home, the rest of our life in fact – we are equals.' She favoured Jamal with an affectionate look. 'But sexually I want him to be my master.

'Poor dear, he is so confused. First I want nothing of the old ways, and then I ask him to make me obey. On the one hand I want freedom, but he must also punish me.'

James listened, astonished, any comment at this stage would have been redundant. This was a situation entirely new to him, but he was beginning to realise, not without possibilities.

Jamal finally found his voice. 'Even when Surinder got me to understand her needs, it wasn't so easy to satisfy them. I consider myself a liberal, not some appalling patriarchal wife beater. I know what she wants but I'm not sure how to proceed. It sounds silly I'm sure, but…' he spread his arms helplessly.

'Not silly at all,' James replied encouragingly. 'I wish more people were as open-minded. Of course, you don't want to really hurt Surinder, nor, if I understand what she has said correctly, does she wish to suffer – and this is the all important part – more than she chooses. For you, Jamal, to fulfil her desires you must be totally believable in your role. May I demonstrate?'

Jamal looked to Surinder. 'But of course, this is why we've invited you,' she replied on behalf of them both.

'Surinder,' his tone was stern and direct, 'your behaviour today has been quite disgraceful; embarrassing Jamal in front of an honoured guest. You deserve to be taught a lesson, do you not?'

She stood before him, head bowed, hands at her sides.

Eventually, after a long pregnant pause, James reached out to lift her chin. Surinder held his gaze defiantly, her eyes flickering with suppressed excitement.

'Yes, master, it is true,' she agreed in a hushed voice. 'I am most wicked, please do as you will.'

Jamal watched, silent, mesmerised.

'Indeed,' James acknowledged, and decisively led her by the arm to an ornately carved, thickly padded footstool. 'I intend to show Jamal how to deal with any such lack of respect in the future, to which end you will forthwith do exactly as you're told. First, remove your sari.'

Languorously, Surinder began to unwind the diaphanous material, revelling in the unashamedly rapt stares of the two men watching her. Slowly, erotically, she slid the length of fine cloth from her body until at last she stood naked, proud and magnificent.

Well, almost naked; ruby-red lips, eyes dark with kohl,

gold bangles on her wrists and rings on her fingers, a glittering nose stud and delicate chains around each ankle and her slender waist. High-heeled sandals and surprisingly slender legs exhibited Surinder's full, firm buttocks, and generous dark-nippled breasts to perfection.

'Kneel on the stool, hands on the floor.'

With a final rebellious glance Surinder obeyed, treating James and Jamal to the sight of toned thighs and gloriously rounded hindquarters.

From his bag James took the trusty tawse that had earlier proved its effectiveness so well, and offered it to an incredulous Jamal.

'It doesn't have to be a tawse,' he explained. 'The palm of your hand is fine, although I think such intimate contact might best be savoured with this minx over your knee. Alternatively, a ruler, hairbrush, wooden spoon or paddle will all do equally well. You'll note that in this position, head well down, weight set forward, Surinder's hands are too busy supporting her body to get in the way.' He ran an approving hand across the delectable bottom, which couldn't be better presented.

'Build up slowly, and as Surinder becomes more aroused so her tolerance of harsher strokes will increase. Want to start?'

'No, you go first,' croaked Jamal. 'I'll watch and learn.'

'Fair enough,' replied James, stepping into position and smoothly swinging the tawse through the air.

The sound of leather cracking upon skin filled the room.

For the next few minutes James alternated from cheek to cheek, ensuring every centimetre received an even dose. Soon Surinder was gasping, twisting her hips in a most beguiling manner. A moist glistening among her dark pubic hair clearly showed the pink glow that toasted her coffee-coloured backside to be producing the desired effect.

'Your turn, I think,' James said, handing the paddle to Jamal, who began to beat the proffered rump with a couple of extremely tentative swipes.

'Not like that, darling,' complained his frustrated spouse. 'Don't be such a wimp.'

Her goading struck exactly the intended chord. With a look of grim determination Jamal began to put years of winning amateur badminton cups to good use, only to stop again, bewildered, at the sound of Surinder's anguished cries.

'Don't stop, please,' she gasped as the smart spread to encompass every centimetre of her nates with a sexually charged inner glow. 'If it gets too much I'll use a code word, "mercy". Otherwise, for once no really does mean yes.'

Eventually, pained more by her awkward pose than her burning behind, Surinder called a halt and climbed red-faced to her feet, kneading her buttocks with both hands. Eyes misty, mouth soft, Surinder dragged Jamal to her, kissing him hungrily.

'That's more like my tiger.' She turned to James eagerly. 'Time for the next part of the lesson?'

'Certainly,' he agreed. 'But that's not something you need me to teach you. Get that sore bottom over the arm of the sofa and let Jamal make it quite clear who's in charge. Perhaps he might try something else from the list of implements I suggested earlier, or maybe he'd prefer to massage some soothing cream into that delicious derriere. Either way the choice is strictly yours. I'll just bid you both farewell. The invoice will be in the post,' he added.

While quickly making a tactful exit from the room, James, from the corner of his eye, saw Jamal grasp his wife's hips and sink his full length into her ready, rapacious sex. Unseen by her newly empowered husband, Surinder mouthed a silent thank you to him as the door closed.

Back in the car James was only too happy to call it a day, when his mobile rang.

'I was just on my way back,' he told Mona.

'I guessed as much, and I'm sorry to be the one to stymie your plans, but I'm afraid the bank manager called. Wants to see you.'

'Oh hell,' James groaned. 'Not Mrs Harrington.'

'I know,' Mona sympathised. 'I do wish dear old Mr Browne hadn't retired. Miss keen-to-make-a-mark-in-the-world is giving us grief about the overdraft.'

'Again,' James said heavily. He was now thoroughly pissed off. 'Mona, are you thinking what I'm thinking?'

'Time to wheel out the emergency plan, you mean? Yes, it looks like it's been kept in reserve long enough. Okay, James, go for it and let's get this bitch off our backs.'

'Too true – see you later.'

Upon entering her bright modern office it seemed from the gorgon-like expression with which she faced him that Mrs Harrington didn't like James, and equally transparently that feeling was reciprocated.

Hell, if she took her professional persona home what must Mr Harrington – who James knew to be a good few years older than his shapely but belligerent wife – suffer?

Mrs Harrington wasn't without her sources of information either, and in the last few months had discovered exactly what kept the wolf from the door of Mona and her carpenter husband. Smugly she'd confronted them with the truth at an earlier meeting, only to suffer the chagrin of a swiftly evaporating triumph when they cheerfully admitted to the professional service James rendered, unashamed and unabashed.

'This overdraft really can't be allowed to continue,' she opened dismissively, without any polite niceties. 'It's gone on longer than the target set by head office.'

'Head office should try coping with the cashflow fluctuations of a small business,' James replied reasonably. 'Anyway, you agreed this loan for the specific purpose of a house extension which is nearly finished. I'm confident we can clear the outstanding balance within three months.'

'Not acceptable,' Mrs Harrington responded firmly.

'And why not?' James ventured without being intimidated.

'I told you, it exceeds the target settlement date set by head office,' she repeated.

'That wouldn't be the target which, should you achieve it, brings the bonus of a company-funded holiday in Florida, would it?' said James archly.

'That is irrelevant.' Despite herself Mrs Harrington's voice rose an octave, betraying her surprise, her guilt implicit in the reply it was now too late to retract.

'I've had quite enough of your bullying, Mrs Harrington,' James attacked before she could re-establish the upper hand, 'and I don't intend to suffer any more of it. I'm sick of insecure middle managers trying to impose their blinkered view on the world, especially when it's from such shaky a foundation as yours.'

'Now listen here—' Mrs Harrington began, her voice tinged with panic as she tried to marshal what fading powers remained to her.

'No, you listen for once,' James cut in with quiet assertiveness. 'I hear things and I keep confidences, but only up to a point.' He paused to look significantly at the increasingly pale figure before him. 'For example, since your husband joined the local freemasons – whether for social advancement or to avoid your shrewish demands I neither know nor care – this bank branch has made some loan decisions which might not bear much examination by your precious head office.' Somehow Mrs Harrington, not normally lost for words, seemed to have lost the power of speech. No longer merely pale, her face turned white while he watched. 'Decisions which might blight a promising career.' He pressed home his advantage. 'You, Mrs Harrington, have over-reached yourself and in order to cover your tracks have been making my life and that of a number of other local small firms hell. But you are now going to turn over a new leaf.'

He stood and walked purposefully to the office door, which he locked. 'I and the other small fry in your portfolio will from hereon be treated fairly – nothing more, we want no special favours, we don't roll up our trouser legs except to paddle in the sea.'

He walked with measured strides back across the office and stood behind her, firmly grasping her shoulders, feeling the muscles, taut with tension, contract beneath her pristine white blouse. 'In return for which your secrets will remain just that, but,' he added, a palpable threat in his voice, 'be aware I have proof of what I say. Try to go back on our agreement and I'll have no hesitation in making the facts public.'

'Agreement?' Mrs Harrington had at last found her voice. 'What agreement?'

'The one we are just about to make. The one in which you undertake to treat my business and others like it with scrupulous fairness.' An unfamiliar sensation of anger surged through his veins. 'After you have been punished for your disgraceful behaviour.'

'P-punished?' she blurted. 'What, you mean physically, here?'

'Most certainly,' James confirmed smoothly. 'I intend to make that pert backside pay the price for the last few months' abuse of your position. Perhaps spending the rest of the day working while standing up will enable you to discover a glimmer of humanity in that sad soul of yours.'

'And if I refuse?' she challenged weakly.

'I'll give you a good hiding anyway and dam the consequences. You may bring me down, but you'll come with me in a flurry of embarrassingly public scrutiny. The tabloids will have a field day.'

'But, no one's ever…'

'No, more's the pity. Nobody has ever confronted you with any consequences since you were a selfish teenage brat; but now that's changed.'

In a flash James hoisted Mrs Harrington upright from her chair, spun her around and draped her unceremoniously over the back, her head pressed into the cushioned seat, wrists pinned to the small of her back.

'Since this is no doubt an unfamiliar position, I shan't be phased if you struggle,' he said laconically, 'but you'll save yourself an awful lot of trouble if you just take what's coming.' Pinning her kegs with one of his own he tugged the tailored skirt to her waist, occasioning a wail of protest in response.

'Shout all you like, your secretary is taking a conveniently long lunch break,' he told her. 'And even if she were here I imagine she'd be offering to help me rather than rescue you.'

Struggling to no avail Mrs Harrington remained firmly bent over the chair, unable to prevent her expensive knickers being drawn to her knees, baring her bottom like some naughty child. Blushing scarlet she moaned in humiliation.

'Not very nice to be permitted no dignity, is it?' said James, while admiring what, it had to be admitted, was an absolute peach of a bottom. Firm and full without being overlarge, and positively demanding to be spanked, Mrs Harrington's immaculate posterior would have been a credit to a woman ten years younger than her twenty-eight years.

Picking up a thick plastic ruler from the adjacent desktop James laid it across his intended target, attractively delineated by ivory-hued suspenders which matched the doffed knickers and the darker bands at the top of the beige stockings fastened to them.

Shriek and attempt to kick though she did, Mrs Harrington had not the slightest chance to protect her exposed posterior from the hardest tanning James had yet delivered. No moderate build up to acclimatise the hitherto uninitiated to the ruler's fierce sting. No intermissions wherein the supplicant might gently massage her burnished cheeks. Rehabilitation might come later; right now retribution was required.

From the uppermost swell of her hips to just above her knees James mercilessly thrashed Mrs Harrington crimson, covering every inch of skin twice, thrice even, with the ruler's unforgiving kiss.

Soon the twin trembling orbs positively radiated heat and James decided to alter his technique, turning the ruler vertically to smack down into the cleft separating her radiant half moons, and then devilishly visiting the sensitive area where buttocks and thigh meld into one.

Skirt bunched around her waist, knickers tangling her high-heeled shoes, hips jerking and weaving at each satisfyingly loud report, tears running in rivulets down her face, Mrs Harrington was defeated.

'All right,' she gasped finally as James mercifully ceased his expertly agonising attentions to her blazing hindquarters. 'I'm sorry, sorry, sorry. You're right; someone should have done this ages ago. I suppose in a way I was half hoping a man would take me to task. Perhaps if I'd married for love instead of money they might. But I never realised anything would hurt this much!'

'Apology accepted. Now, do we have an agreement?' James enquired sternly.

'We have an agreement,' she confirmed contritely,

'which I'll even put into writing. I'll reform, I promise; do better, change, anything but take a further thrashing. I can't take any more.'

'Oh, but you will,' said James. 'First you get rid of the skirt and knickers. Second you stand bare-bummed and tearful by your desk and write that agreement in your own fair hand. Then last but not least you'll go to the centre of the room, bend right over, spread your legs and grasp your ankles and take six hard strokes from my belt.'

And Mrs Harrington did. Shakily she wrote the binding document, which James tucked into his pocket with a smile of satisfaction. Then, mustering all the dignity and poise possible under the circumstances, she assumed the required position, mortifyingly aware that every inch of her vagina and anus were open to the scrutiny of her confident, dominating, adversary.

Ultimately Mrs Harrington summoned the strength to bear up bravely under the final onslaught to her well-whipped buttocks, counting each fiery lash of the leather in a firm clear voice, and not even seeking to demur when James prudently photographed the end result as an insurance against future backsliding.

And as he bent to retrieve her clothes from the floor, he was astonished to notice the abundantly damp evidence of desire glistening on Pamela Harrington's sex.

Tentatively he ran a hand across her burning haunches, letting his fingertips brush against the moist mons, hearing her moans, this time fuelled by passion instead of pain in response to his gentle touch.

'I don't suppose…?' she ventured huskily.

'And you're right not too,' James answered, with a

twinge of regret and a lump rather lower than in his throat. 'Not that I'm not tempted,' he added honestly, 'but that's not part of the personal service I offer. And in any case, that hiding was strictly to punish, not pleasure you. But at least now you can better appreciate the attractions of a little chastisement. Go on; goad that spineless social-climbing husband of yours into first thrashing then fucking you properly. Better still; find someone else to look after your needs. Lose some of those frustrations and get a life.'

'I just might, James, I just might,' she said pensively, standing stiffly and gingerly rubbing her blotchy rear while he made his exit. 'Oh, and thank you.'

Hot and exhausted James was glad to be finally home. Nice work if you can get it, but right now he was bushed; a shower and a beer were his sole priorities.

'Good day at the office, dear?' Mona asked – it was their private joke.

'Not bad. I managed to sort out the problem at the bank. I don't think well have any more trouble there. So yes, overall a good day. Just a bit on the tiring side.'

'Well done my conquering hero,' Mona smiled. 'Now, not too tired, I hope?' she added, wrapping her arms around his neck to deliver a homecoming kiss.

James smelt her perfume, felt the warmth of her slim body, firm breasts, nipples erect beneath the skimpy top.

'No,' he answered warily. 'Why?'

'Because,' she grinned impishly, tilting her head to one side, 'I'm afraid I've been rather naughty.'

Mona bent provocatively to brush imaginary specks of dust from her knee-length boots, her short leather shirt sliding up to reveal her sex, smooth and completely shaven since this morning, and devoid of the protection of any semblance of underwear. 'I seem to have mislaid tomorrow's worksheets,' she said with a provocative pout. 'I can't think what you're going to do with me.'

James could. Tired he might be, but inside that old magic stirred. 'I think you're going to be dealt with most severely,' he growled.

Postman

'I can't understand it, you think he'd welcome a change.'

The new sorting office foreman watched, puzzled, while in the yard outside the window Tony Meadows climbed into the familiar red van with all the appearance of a man happy at his work.

'I know,' replied his colleague, pouring two mugs of tea, 'it's a mystery to me, too. Always the same round; you know he's done that route since he started five years ago.'

'Doesn't he get ever bored?' enquired the new foreman.

'Nope, seems to love every minute; claims to be "integrated with the community". Plays merry hell if we try to move him and then we get the union on our backs.'

'Does a good job, though. Definitely popular with the punters. A regular Postman Pat. In fact, we have more complimentary letters about Tony than the rest of the division combined.'

'Ah well, I'm for a quiet life. If it ain't broke don't fix it, and after all, "every unhappy customer tells nine other people",' stated the foreman, mimicking the latest Post Office advertising campaign. 'Best let things be, if you ask me. Pass the sugar.'

Tony whistled cheerfully as he drove through the Cotswold countryside. The warm early autumn sun cast a mellow light across carefully tended fields, interspersed with trees tinged with yellow and gold. For all that the view was familiar Tony never tired of it; there must be thousands who'd give their right arm to have his job, and that's without knowing about the perks. You wouldn't make your fortune as a rural postie, that's for sure, but when it came to quality of life, well, Tony reckoned himself fortunate indeed.

Not that he was usually given to such introspective reveries; Tony felt life was for living and opportunities there to be grasped. No trendy counselling or therapies for him; he'd long ago developed the perfect strategies to relieve stress and imbue the familiar patterns of day-to-day living with meaning.

A few minutes later he was parked in a lay-by on the edge of a picture book, mellow-yellow stone built country town where he paused to check the day's letters and packages.

Aha, a parcel for Mrs Hardwick at The Hall. He'd not reach there until after lunch, but that was certainly very promising. Meanwhile, more mundane deliveries awaited.

He drove to the square at the town's centre and, having carefully locked Her Majesty's mail conveyance, began his familiar morning delivery beat at the teashop on the high street.

The *Copper Kettle* wasn't open to the public at this hour, but Tony had acquired the habit of stopping for a cuppa with Molly Prine, the proprietor, while her staff prepared for the mid-morning coffee rush.

Molly was seated at her usual table in the back of the shop. A woman of what the French charmingly term, 'a certain age', she still possessed a trim-waisted, well-rounded figure topped by a flawless, high-cheeked face. Such lines as there were around her eyes gave her the allure of one who has savoured much of the considerable best life's physical pleasures have to offer. And yet, despite her welcoming smile, this morning Molly's forehead was creased with concern.

'You look fed up, Molly,' Tony said.

'Oh, not really, it's just that the new waitress has gone and dropped a perfectly good tea set.'

'Susie Trip?' asked Tony. 'I can't say I'm surprised, she always was a bit of a dreamer, that one.'

'Not a bad girl, mind,' said Molly, kindly. 'Quite a willing worker, in fact – when her mind's not full of some fantasy or other.'

She sat back, crossing her shapely legs to afford Tony an ample view of nylon clad thighs, and impishly aware of the effort it took him to divert his gaze. They sat in contemplative silence for a moment.

'A prime case for your own unique brand of staff discipline, I'd have thought,' Tony offered at last, with a conspiratorial smile.

'Without a doubt,' agreed Molly. 'But therein lies the second problem of the day; I twisted my wrist this morning lifting a crate of milk.' She looked directly at Tony and he, never slow on the uptake, was quick to interpret her gaze.

'You want me to…?'

Molly raised her eyebrows in mute reply. My, but she was still an attractive woman, thought Tony, wistfully. There had been a time, oh, it must be almost twenty years before, when he'd had occasion to take a much younger

144

but equally shapely Ms Prine to task. The recollection was an extremely pleasant one.

They'd been out on what for Tony had rapidly become the date from hell. No matter what he did, what he said, Molly always retorted with some shrewish reply. He smiled ruefully at his own naïveté. With the benefit of hindsight it was all so obvious. Ultimately, patience exhausted, exasperated beyond caring, he'd pulled the little minx across his lap for a thoroughly deserved bare-bottomed spanking, followed of course by a tearful, on her part, and extremely energetic on his, *rapprochement*. And throughout Tony had actually believed himself to be in charge.

Despite subsequently understanding that Molly had skilfully engineered the entire situation it had, he recalled, been something of an epiphany. Indeed it was no exaggeration to say their brief encounter had changed his life irrevocably. Once Tony had tasted the delights of applying his hand to the taut curves of young Molly's utterly delightful bottom cheeks, and experienced the passionate vigour of their subsequent coupling, there was no going back to the vanilla life of before. Fortunately he was not without charm, and over the years a succession of comely women had proved willing to accept a spanking, and more often than not, a great deal more. Which answered the question posed by so many female customers on his regular route: Why hadn't he ever married? Variety for Tony was not just the spice, but also the very stuff of life.

Molly's voice gently coaxed him back to reality. 'Only if you've time. I know it's an imposition but, well, Susie already knows what she's in for, so it seems cruel to keep her waiting. And you're such a familiar face around here.'

'No problem, glad to help,' said Tony affably, doing a good job of concealing his glee. 'is Susie here now?'

'Yes, out the back polishing cutlery.'

'What say I borrow your office, then?'

A few short minutes later saw Tony sitting, stern-faced and commanding, on a chair in Molly's modest office, well away from the main tearooms in an extension to the rear of the shop. In front of him, fingers clasped nervously before her, eyes set resolutely at the floor, stood a young waitress with glimmering green eyes and tied-back, auburn hair, dressed demurely in the white apron and black dress of her calling, and little white cap perched incongruously on top of her head.

'Well, Susie,' he began in measured, compelling, but not unkind tones, 'you knew the penalty for misdemeanours when you took the job. Molly's always been quite open with her girls about what to expect if they persist in stupid mistakes.'

'Yes,' mumbled the poor girl.

'Honestly, you're nineteen now and supposed to be earning your own living,' Tony continued briskly. 'You really must learn to concentrate; perhaps a short sharp shock will bring you to your senses.'

'Yes, sir.' Susie forced a nervous smile. 'I know, sir, and I'd rather be spanked than have my pay docked...'

The sentence was left unfinished as, apprehensive and uncertain, Susie struggled to find the right words. Knowing full well the value of silence, Tony sat impassively as she fidgeted before him, eventually finding her voice.

'Um, Mrs Prine said she'd hurt her wrist, so you'd be doing it. That's all right, but…' Susie's voice trailed off into silence again, her feet shuffling aimlessly.

'But what?' Tony pressed, adopting his most severe countenance.

'Well, I've never been, you know, spanked before,' she confessed, with an innocence that made his cock pulse. 'Will it hurt much?'

'Well, if it didn't hurt there'd be precious little point to it,' Tony said reasonably.

'You couldn't, you know, just this one time, let me off with a warning?' Worth a try, although by now Susie clearly knew in her heart this bid for clemency was doomed.

'You've had warnings a plenty,' Tony replied coldly, relishing the moment. 'And if you don't get yourself across my knee here and *now*, the only thing left is the sack.'

With a miserable sniff of defeat Susie shuffled forward, offered no resistance when laid across his knees, and lay meekly as Tony prepared her for punishment. The short black skirt rode up to expose svelte, coltish thighs, and Tony savoured the sight appreciatively before tugging it to her waist. Lacy white knickers complemented two splendidly rounded orbs, neatly encased in her shiny, honey-toned tights.

Nothing was ever gained by rushing; indeed, the stately process of the spanking ritual was an inherent part of its charm, depending on one's perspective of course. He ran his palms lightly across the proffered cheeks, enjoying the feel of nubile flesh.

'If we're going to do this properly it'll have to be on

the bare,' he declared decisively. Susie groaned, but compliantly lifted her hips, allowing him to pull the skimpy items down almost to her knees.

Smack!

His palm tested the resilience of the plump cheeks, and discovered them to be soft yet well sprung.

Smack! Smack! Smack!

With a steadying hand in the small of her back Tony employed the other to gradually build up a percussive cadence. Each slap carefully judged, neither too harsh nor too tentative, stinging but not yet searing, alternating from cheek to cheek, slowly circling the entire surface of her posterior and certainly not neglecting the curve of Susie's hips nor the tender backs of her upper thighs.

After the first minute or two Susie began to breath more heavily, then groaned and gasped until she was wriggling animatedly on his lap, toes pivoting on one side, fingers urgently gripping the chair legs for purchase on the other. His hand started to smart, but not nearly as much as Susie's beet-red bum; he was a practised judge of such matters.

Smack! Smack! Smack!

Jiggling hips moving rhythmically with each successive slap, she ground her pelvis hard against his uniform serge covered knees, clearly confused by her urgent need to seek release for another wholly unexpected yet equally intense sensation, which complemented the pain. Susie's protests became more vocal but, like her increasingly animated attempts to escape his grasp, seemed more as if she were playing out her allotted role than seriously trying to bring the punishment to a conclusion. Perversely, sensually, her thighs parted, treating Tony to glimpses of wispy, glistening curls and pink, engorged lips.

He employed the full range of his expertise; slightly cupping his hand to catch the full rounded swell of her under-cheeks, then switching to a series of lateral skimming strikes across the burnished surface of her skin, employing just the upper joints of his fingers to do so and yielding a most satisfyingly loud report.

Next he reverted to alternating from side to side, peach to peach, but employed the trusty technique of delivering three or four rapid impacts in quick succession, all in exactly the same spot, a gambit guaranteed to ratchet up the distress ratio of the unfortunate bottom's wretched owner. Finally a little craftsmanship; attention to detail, filling in any hitherto neglected spots – showing as anything other than a bright crimson – plus cruel smacks into the bottom cleft and across the oh so tender area where bottom and thighs so delightfully meet.

'Last six,' he announced, giving Susie her cue, and determined to make sure she felt each and every one. Her scorched buttocks rose to meet his hardened palm, hips humping in an unconscious physical parody of her innermost desires until, with something between a shriek and a moan, she slumped limply across his lap, tears in her eyes, cheeks almost equally as flushed as her beaten buttocks. But strangely, something approaching a contrite smile adorned her pretty face.

Tony politely made no reference to this orgasmic denouement but waited patiently, gently stroking the hot-to-the-touch buttocks while Susie regained her composure. Eventually he helped her clamber dreamily to her feet, watching as she gingerly pulled up her knickers and tights over a bottom which would stay hot and sore for several hours yet.

'Thank you, sir, I needed that,' Susie said with ambiguity as she walked slowly towards the door. She turned on the threshold. 'Perhaps I won't need to daydream so much in future, will I?' She grinned wickedly. 'Oh, and I did take care to choose a teapot that was already cracked.'

And with that she walked stiffly out of the office, leaving Tony to reflect that in twenty years some things had changed very little.

His next delivery was to a delicatessen a couple of hundred yards further along the same thoroughfare. He entered, whistling cheerfully, but scarcely had the chance to take a step further before being struck on the shoulder by a flying spoon.

'Ow!' he exclaimed, surprised rather than pained by the fleeting impact.

'Oh no,' a Mediterranean face, stunningly pretty and framed by a shock of shoulder-length, raven black curls, appeared at the rear of the premises. 'Oh, Tony, I'm terribly sorry, I thought you were Pete.'

'Which would have made it all right?' he said, rubbing his shoulder.

'No, it certainly wouldn't,' Pete said sternly from the other side of the small shop, scowling. 'You and your Italian temper, Carla. Just look what you've done.' The intended target of his young wife's wrath turned to Tony apologetically. 'Getting this shop up and running is turning out to be tougher than we thought, Tony,' he added, by way of partial explanation. 'I'm beginning to think that living and working together might not be such a clever idea. Carla's been in a foul mood all morning. God, when she's like this I could cheerfully put her across my knee...' He shrugged hopelessly.

'Then why don't you?' snapped Carla, eyes blazing fiercely. 'You're supposed to be the boss. In Italy most small concerns are family run, but we don't have such problems. But then in Italy we are not so repressed as you English.'

'But,' Pete hesitated, 'this is the year two thousand; we're supposed to be equal partners – in marriage and business.'

'Huh, English stiff upper lip,' Carla sneered. 'About the only thing that is stiff around here,' she added provocatively.

'If I might make a suggestion...' The warring couple's eyes turned in unison to the momentarily forgotten Tony, now recovered from his ordeal in the crossfire and speaking in a quietly authoritative tone. 'As the temporarily aggrieved third party...' he waved away further repentance from Carla and Pete, '...no, hear me out. I think you've got your cultural wires crossed. If I'm correct, what Carla's trying to say is that displays of temper followed by rapid retribution were part of her upbringing. No one's suggesting you become a wife beater Pete, but it seems to me that if you are going to continue living and working together in anything approaching harmony, you're going to have to dominate this tempestuous spitfire.'

Hands on hips, Carla drew herself up to her full five foot four, nodded approvingly and added her voice to Tony's argument: 'Rows are better solved with passion, not sulking. Be unreasonable if you have to be, but spare me the simmering resentment.'

'See what I mean?' said Tony, as if that settled the debate. 'There's obviously still room in this world for a man who can deal firmly with a feisty partner.'

The idea had clearly taken root, but Pete's English reserve remained uppermost and he made no move.

'Since I was the one on the receiving end of that outburst, perhaps I could demonstrate?' Tony suggested.

'Of course.' Further reminded of his wife's embarrassing behaviour and still not fully appreciating what lay behind Tony's request, Pete agreed.

And to his astonishment, the postman quickly flipped the closed sign on the door and drew the blinds, pulled the fiery Latin beauty towards him, effortlessly wrapping Carla around his hip and pinning her across his upper thigh. Arms pinned helplessly, feet clear of the floor, true to her temperament Carla kicked and struggled, but Tony was more than a match for her lithe form and he held her firmly; tight leather trousers showcasing every inch of her small but deliciously prominent bottom. Then, managing to pick up the wooden spoon she'd shied in his direction, he set about making the punishment fit the crime.

Crack! *Crack*! *Crack*!

Pete stared open-mouthed as Carla received a long overdue spanking. Rooted to the spot, it somehow never occurred to him to intervene, to stop the postman from walloping his young wife's shapely behind. And to his further amazement, after only a couple of minutes Carla seemed to meekly accept her fate, the squeals of protest diminished, her high-heeled sandals ceased to flail the air, and she no longer struggled against Tony's grip, instead hanging onto his legs for support while her rapidly warming hindquarters squirmed in response to every stinging impact.

Tony took advantage of the protective covering to lay on some really hard strokes, expertly tanning the leather and thus the supple olive-toned skin beneath. Thwack after noisy thwack echoed around the small shop as cowhide and wood made painful contact. His stance may have been unorthodox, but it had the distinct advantage of allowing Tony to savour the sensuous feel of Carla's pert breasts – nipples perceptibly stiffening – pressed warmly against him as he held her determinedly *in situ*.

'You'll need to develop your own technique of course,' he said to her dumbstruck husband without pausing. Taking it as a *fait accompli* that he would henceforth bring an element of physical discipline to his marriage, Tony offered a little sage advice. 'As far as possible, always begin with an old-fashioned hand spanking. Don't be in too much of a rush to get her knickers off, but always finish on the bare. Not only does this make it crystal clear you'll stand no nonsense, but it warms their arse nicely and makes it more receptive for a dose of the strap, cane, or whatever's your favourite.

'Take no notice of pleading and snivelling, and don't be fooled by a few tears. Careful of the coccyx at the top of the buttocks, and go sparingly on her sensitive thighs if you want her to be receptive rather than resentful once you've finished. Have I missed anything, Carla?'

'Oh… no, I think you know just how to handle a girl,' gasped the struggling Italian, as he continued to beat out a tattoo on her beautiful behind.

Eventually he stopped, laid down the spoon and draped a thoroughly chastened Carla face down over the padded top of a high stool by the delicatessen's counter, her groans mingling discomfort and disappointment in equal measure.

'Let's see the result,' he commanded. For an instant she glared defiantly at the two men, then, with an insouciant Latin shrug, her hands ceased their ruefully rubbing and tugged the tight leather down over the inviting swell of her hips. Glorying in their captivated gaze, she deliberately made a solo performance of the tantalisingly slow revelation of her castigated cheeks. Underneath the hugging trousers Carla wore nothing but a slender black thong, neatly bisecting her glowing, ruby-red globes and barely concealing her visibly wet sex.

Tony handed the spoon to Pete. 'I suggest you continue. An excellent piece of work in progress, though I say so myself, but Carla would benefit no end from a further good hard smacking of that insolent little bare bottom. Then, when she's properly subdued, the two of you might find her position has other possibilities…'

Pete's face portrayed a look of determination. As if adjusting to the feel of new clothes and deciding he did indeed like the fit, he proceeded with an assured sense of purpose. 'You know, I think you're right, I should have done this a long time ago.' Turning to Carla he barked his instructions. 'Get right over that stool, young lady. Stick that bottom up where I can thrash it properly and hang on to the legs – you won't be sitting down again today.' Purposefully he began to tug the trousers down over her calves and shoes, and there was no doubt the skimpy thong would soon follow.

'I'll leave you to it,' said Tony, tactfully making for the door, where he glanced back just in time to catch Carla surreptitiously favouring him with a dazzling smile, and as he popped a package through the letterbox next door the sound of energetic slapping was music to his ears.

Rain had begun to fall when Tony finally drove up the lengthy gravel drive to the palatial Georgian mansion that was Hardwick Hall, and the last call of the day. But it would take more than a little rain to dampen his spirits. A bundle of letters in one hand, a long slim parcel in the other, he reached the imposing front door just as it opened and a soft-toned feminine voice beckoned him enter.

'Tony, lovely to see you. Don't stay on the threshold getting wet, come on in.'

Caught unawares, Tony stopped dead in his tracks; this was hardly the reception he'd anticipated. The lady of the manor, Clarissa, was not attired as he had ever seen her before. The blue dress was short, sleeveless, tailored from latex, and fitted Clarissa's hourglass figure like the proverbial glove.

An elegant lady approaching forty, Clarissa was fortunate in having the time and money to keep her extremely curvaceous body in the sort of perfect condition a woman ten years her junior would envy; a testimony to the power of diet, rigorous exercise, and the desire to thwart the depredations of time.

And what a pair of legs, thought Tony, reluctantly shifting his unashamedly hungry gaze from the voluptuous swell of her hips. Her back towards the postman, Clarissa sashayed across the large hall, the seams of her black stockings mesmerising him even further. She turned to face him and her eyes dropped for a second, to the prominent bulge in the front of Tony's uniform trousers.

'Postmen don't carry guns, do they?' she mused, placing the letters dismissively aside.

'No,' he blurted, 'and the lady of the house doesn't usually answer the door, does she?'

'*Touché*,' replied the delightful Mrs Hardwick. 'They do when the housekeeper has been given the day off. This may be a substantial country pile, but we no longer have retinues of staff, I'm afraid.'

'Nevertheless,' Tony nodded significantly at the lady of the manor's choice of apparel, 'you appear to be expecting to, er, entertain someone.'

'Quite,' responded the lady, totally unflustered, and then her voice dropped a tone as she moved gracefully forward and draped slender arms seductively around his neck. 'It gets so terribly boring here on my own sometimes and, since you have something of a reputation around here, Mr Postman, I think it's high time I discovered the secrets of your special delivery service.'

'Hang on a minute,' said Tony, inhaling her heady perfume, but nevertheless disentangling himself from the unsolicited embrace. 'You're taking rather too much for granted for my liking. Just because you're lady of the manor doesn't give you automatic rights over us mere mortals. Besides,' he added pointedly, 'I'm not the only one around here with a reputation.'

She stopped short, a smile dancing playfully over her glistening lips. 'For what, exactly?'

'I think you'll find the answer might be in that package

I've just delivered,' he said. 'Let's have a look, shall we?'

Taking the parcel from the bemused lady he tore at the wrapping. 'You must have ordered this specially,' he breathed, pausing for effect before fully opening the package. 'Perhaps you were rather hoping to find someone to test it?' He held a beautifully made, leather bound riding crop, flexing and bending it between his hands, as she watched with wide hazel eyes.

'Word has it you're extremely practised in such matters,' Tony went on. 'Do you think after years of traipsing up your drive I haven't worked out the contents of some of the strangely shaped packages I've had to deliver? Haven't discover the magazines the plain packaging of which is sometimes "accidentally" torn at the sorting office? I'm discrete, Mrs Hardwick, but I'm not dumb.'

'Word also has it I'm not the only one who's experienced in "such matters", as you so coyly put it,' Clarissa countered, unfazed by the implications of Tony's statement.

'Tell me, do you have an aversion to nouns?' she continued. 'Is there a problem with stating openly what we both know we're talking about. Spanking, corporal punishment; is that so difficult to say?'

'Not difficult, no,' Tony said, 'but in a close knit rural community, probably unwise. What's acceptable in London is still open to misinterpretation in these conservative parts. Wasn't your husband once a local magistrate?'

'Until his death, yes, and like most of his peers, a right old hypocrite he was too,' Clarissa scoffed. 'Condemning in public what he privately enjoyed. But that was then, this is now, and I don't think either of us is in any danger of misinterpreting the situation, are we?

'Which is why,' she continued huskily, segueing back into brazen temptress mode, 'I've taken the liberty of preparing the sitting room. Please do follow me.'

The room was on a grand scale but comfortably furnished, and Clarissa had prudently closed the heavy chenille curtains. A thickly padded chaise longue occupied the centre, discreetly lit by lamps and the flames of a blazing log fire. 'Well,' she said seductively, handing him the crop, 'I think you know what's required.'

Tony's demeanour changed abruptly, from avuncular to angry. 'I'll decide what's required. You may be used to giving orders, have spent a lifetime, however benevolently, issuing commands, but you can't just snap your fingers and have me meekly follow,' he said harshly.

'Oh, so I'm the figure of power, am I?' she replied defiantly. 'Do you foolishly think life for a woman in my position is really that different from that endured by any other woman? Aren't our men every bit as domineering? Arrogantly self-confident and convinced of their divine right to be in charge, they seldom feel the need to indulge trite liberal sentiments of equality or indulge PC attitudes to the empowerment of women, I can tell you.

'My late husband,' she added, almost nostalgically, 'made it quite abundantly clear who wore the trousers, right from the very start. A good few years younger than him, I'm afraid I really was the archetypal blushing, virgin bride. A closeted upbringing, private preps and boarding school left me quite unprepared for the ways of the world in general, and his demands in particular. For many years I simply thought all men behaved as he did, putting his wife and young female staff to the rod,' she paused meaningfully, 'both sorts of rod… What I never anticipated for a moment, was when he was gone quite how much I'd miss it.'

'Then you won't have any problem doing as you're told,' Tony said firmly. 'And to start with, you can take off that outrageous dress.'

As if expecting nothing less, Clarissa fixed him with a pointed stare then quickly reached behind her back, struggled with a hidden zip and, not without effort, wriggled the brief, shiny garment alluringly down over her hips, undulating before him like a snake shedding its skin, before finally flicking the rubber frock across the polished parquet floor with her toe.

'Free your breasts,' he ordered.

A push-up bra was teasingly removed; revealing mouth-watering breasts, and darkly erect nipples pierced by small gold rings.

'Bare your bottom.'

In response to this further pre-emptory instruction, Clarissa added a note of novelty by executing a full pirouette as she lowered her delicate silk briefs to her trim ankles, before delicately stepping out of the scrap of shimmering material.

'Hands on your head.'

Polished red fingernails shone through her fashionably cut and expensively streaked mane as Tony made a laconic circuit around his compliant victim.

'You've been wicked,' it wasn't a question.

'Yes, sir,' Clarissa agreed readily, eyes sparkling

mischievously.

'Exactly, how?'

'Lascivious thoughts,' she confessed. 'Rather a lot of them, in fact; so much so that I've rather neglected my late husband's estate.'

Tony flicked the crop across the luscious contours of her breasts, the flexible tip lightly touching nipples already engorged with desire. 'I'm sure the lord of the manor would've known how to deal with such dilatory behaviour.'

'Oh, yes indeed.' Clarissa's heavy-lidded eye's briefly closed as she shuddered at the memory.

'And your further wicked ways?' Tony prompted.

'I've been clubbing in London – fetish clubs. Hardly the behaviour of a respectable widow. Think of the scandal, should it become public.'

'Quite,' he agreed, transferring the crop's attentions lower down with a series of sharp, stinging licks across her buttocks, 'but I think we can manage to keep it our secret.' Each recklessly hard swipe of the crop scored a livid red blur on the lustrous expanse of flesh and drew a sharp intake of breath from the lady.

'Oh yes,' Clarissa gazed at him imploringly, the tip of her tongue peeking sensually between parted red lips, 'I really would be *so* grateful.'

'Oh, you will be,' Tony replied with calm assurance, and with a hint of cruelty aimed a number of strokes at her thighs, front and back, scalding the firm flesh between crotch and stocking tops. Clarissa squealed and squirmed, dancing on the spot, livid red stripes burnishing her perfect skin, twisting in a vain attempt to avoid the crop, now cutting across the twin moons of her buttocks. Her gyrations caused her legs to part and, half hidden by fair downy curls, Tony caught the glint of the golden rings decorating her labia.

'An interesting variation on a theme of family jewels,' he observed wryly.

'His lordship liked them,' Clarissa said simply.

'And you…?'

'There's a certain frisson to be had in attending charity events with ladies who lunch, all the time knowing beneath my sensible twin-set are adornments which would cause them to choke on their aperitifs.

Tony took the nipple rings between his fingers and none too gently tugged them, stretching the sensitive tips of her luscious breasts. 'When clubbing, they must be a positive asset…' he mused.

'Like a badge of identity, a shorthand expression of one's desires, it helps to cut to the chase with the male or female of your choice,' Clarissa agreed shamelessly.

'Hmm, bisexuality, I'm not sure this part of middle England's quite ready to accept that yet,' he remarked.

'I think you'll find certain members of the local catering trade quite amenable to the occasional dalliance,' Clarissa said, a trifle smugly.

'If I recall our mail, you've accounts at the new delicatessen and Molly Prine's tearoom?' he questioned.

'Yes, yes,' she gasped, wincing as Tony remorselessly continued to torture her tender breasts.

'So the names Molly and Carla are not unfamiliar to you?'

'Nor to each other…' she answered libidinously.

Filing such priceless information away for future use, Tony propelled her backwards on unsteady high heels until she leant against a heavy Edwardian chair, then, reluctantly relinquishing his hold on her lovely breasts, dropped to his knees to investigate the jewellery piercing the lips of her succulently enticing cunt.

The heavy gold rings glistened with Clarissa's juices; she was so wet to the touch. Her breath came in harsh, panting gasps, her body tight as a bowstring, hips thrust insolently forward. Sliding his thumb into her sopping portal his finger deftly manipulated the rings, pulling insistently at labia engorged with the promise of sex still to come.

'Oooooh,' Clarissa gave an elongated, animal moan of pleasure that increased in timbre as Tony's fingers were aided and abetted by the skilful application of his tongue. Fingers entwined through the rings, he tugged her pubis forward, at the same time thrusting his thumb deeper into her vagina, taking the erect clitoris carefully between his teeth, all the while laving her hot little muff with his probing tongue.

Her voice rose by several octaves as his other hand crept around to roughly pinch her throbbing buttocks, and a finger, slick with juices from her sex, slid across her perineum and teased the tight little bud of her bottom.

'No,' she whimpered in feeble, half-hearted protest; held fast by the rings, barely able to move much less escape, she clearly knew what must inevitably come next.

And her intuition proved correct. Pushing inexorably against the muscles of her anus, he forced his finger fully into her rear passage. Held fast, digitally impaled front and rear, Tony's tongue playing havoc around her inner lips, Clarissa could only moan and twist futilely in response. 'Oh my... oh, don't stop,' she moaned appreciatively.

Far from stopping, Tony increased the speed of his finger fucking, expertly reaming both her tight little passages, the better to prepare them to accommodate his rock hard cock. Moaning all the while, Clarissa's uninhibited excitement helped lubricate his efforts even further, evidence of her excitement coating her thighs.

'What do you deserve, woman?' he asked rhetorically.

'A sound thrashing, sir,' she replied instantly, voice thickly charged with passion.

'And?' For the first and only time Tony raised his voice.

'A really good screw, please sir,' Clarissa added quickly.

'A really good screw,' he repeated, goading her. 'And what, pray tell, might that entail?'

'It will entail your big cock stretching my tight little aristocratic fanny to the limit,' she groaned, eyes glazed, consuming sexual desire pushing her to the point of recklessness. 'Thrust deep inside me so hard, and I don't think I'll be able to take it all. But even if I plead for mercy you'll still fill me to the hilt.'

'And what makes you think my prick's so large?'

'A small but no doubt representative survey reveals the ladies of the village hold you in high regard, master,' Clarissa giggled, despite her predicament. 'Molly Prine seemed most impressed,' she added.

'Does she indeed?' retorted Tony, smiling despite the sexual tension of the moment. 'I can see another visit to the tearoom is required.

'It also appears,' he added, 'that the monstrous regiment hereabouts has a most efficient grapevine. So, in order that you've all got something to talk about in future you, Mrs Hardwick, can get across the end of that chaise longue right now.'

Clarissa obeyed, almost tripping on the vertiginous heels in her haste.

'That's it, head down on the cushion, bottom raised where I can attend to it.' He fussed for several minutes, arranging Clarissa to his satisfaction; hips supported on the generously upholstered arm, knees bent and tucked under the overhang, the better to thrust her lovely rump into prominence. Clarissa's hands remained clasped behind her head.

'Twelve strokes,' he announced when ready, 'and every one a scorcher. I fully intend to leave marks on these plump globes that'll linger for days.'

In reality he intended no such thing; this was erotic chastisement, not assault, but he knew the power words have to stimulate and arouse.

'Stay in position and count each one, after strokes three and nine I shall permit a brief respite, at the halfway point you may rub. Now push that bottom up and out and relax your buttocks.'

For all her hitherto coquettish behaviour, Clarissa's anxiety was almost palpable as she waited in silence for the beating to commence. Measuring his distance, Tony tapped her posterior lightly with the crop, laying the gleaming, supple, leather bound rod of correction across the full width of her orbs. Clarissa wriggled uneasily; a whimper of fear escaped her lips, yet she made no attempt to shift from the humiliating, wholly subservient stance in which he'd placed her. Bottom up, exposed and fully accessible, her upper class confidence quickly faded as the undignified vulnerability of her position became all too apparent.

Tony raised his arm, kept it aloft for several eerily silent seconds, then brought the crop whistling down in an elegantly accurate parabola; skilfully bisecting the fullest part of the proffered posterior with a horizontal line of blazing fire.

A loud crack shattered the quiet, her flesh indented with the impact, then at once sprang back to its original curvaceous dimensions, now adorned by a long, almost luminous welt flanked by two rapidly emerging parallel lines. A sound, somewhere between a wail and sob, escaped Clarissa's lips. The ordeal had begun.

Tony was as good as his word, each successive wheal, skilfully and directly aligned with the first, seared across unblemished flesh, leaving line after blazing line. Slowly the heat generated by each singular stinging blow began to spread across the entire expanse of her soundly whipped globes, gradually culminating into a deep heat that spread to infuse the very core of her sex. All the while she moaned and pleaded, jerked at each impact, drummed her feet and clutched wildly at the seat cushion.

After three Tony soothed the scorched cheeks with his palm, exploring the results of his handiwork with an almost academic interest, drawing a finger across the wet lips between her legs, teasing each opening in turn.

After six he allowed a tearful Clarissa an interlude to stand and massage her rosy-red, ravaged buttocks, taking advantage of the moment to stoop and roll each achingly aroused nipple between his lips, mixing pleasure with the pain, teasing and tormenting.

After nine skilfully applied strokes, none yet

overlapping – though they could have, had he so intended – he spread her legs wide, parted her labia once more and ground hard against her swollen clitoris with a work-hardened palm. Clarissa moaned loudly, thrusting her hips back lewdly, lost in sexual abandon, quiescent to his any and every desire.

Once the promised total of twelve searing stripes had marked her from upper buttocks to stocking tops, Tony stopped, waited until Clarissa's ragged breaths had returned to something approaching normal, then carefully, reverently laid the very tip of the crop against her sex lips. Clarissa's gasp of surprise soon turned to a low moan of pleasure as she guessed Tony's intention.

With the merest flick of the wrist he tapped the leather flap at the crop's slender tip against the sopping lips. And again, yet again, the soft leather softly spanked the engorged flesh. Eyes wide open, mouth forming a perfect O, Clarissa matched each circumspect pat to her naked nates with a tiny cry, one part distress to one part ecstasy. Abruptly changing direction and flicking from left to right, Tony snapped the crop against the exquisitely tender skin of her inner thighs, a sharp reminder of his power to dispense castigation as easily as gratification. Then, as Clarissa's wails and kicking legs displayed her distress, Tony resumed his delicate chastisement of her overheated pussy.

'There's nothing like a good cropping to prepare a girl for sex,' he said, reaching down to free his rampant manhood. Asking no permission, indulging in no foreplay, he tossed the crop aside, grasped Clarissa's hips and thrust his length fully into her aching cunt with a single, savage stroke.

'N-not so much a gun in your pocket… as a *rifle*,' she groaned, thrusting her hips back to meet him. 'Oh, that's lovely – deep and hard.'

'Take every inch, Mrs Hardwick, enjoy it while you can,' he grunted enigmatically, shafting steadily, taking her to the very brink of orgasm, only to withdraw at the penultimate second, then bearing down hard upon her ravaged rear once again.

'But for a woman of your position, special deliveries must come via the tradesman's entrance…'

Paying the Price

'You paid how much?' Callum paced the floor in exasperation, while Sue, the object of his wrath, defiantly stood her ground.

'I paid fifteen hundred pounds, which is a bargain. That's what January sales are for. Reduced by fifty percent for the sake of a barely visible scuffmark. Hell, Callum, we could never otherwise have afforded a piece this good.' She gestured towards the sofa, standing lonely and, by Callum at least, unloved in the centre of the half decorated room. 'It's a lovely contemporary piece by a designer usually way out of our price range. Go on, you have to admit you like it,' she said.

'Yes,' agreed Callum, making a visible effort to remain calm and rational, 'of course I like it, but it doesn't automatically follow that you should have made the purchase if we can't afford it, and anyway, since when was want synonymous with need? This isn't about taste, Sue, it's about cost. Sure, it'll look great in the room, if we can ever find the money for minor details such as floor coverings or to finish decorating.' He shrugged angrily. 'It's not as if we even talked about buying the damn thing first.'

'Oh, don't be so tight-arsed,' Sue snapped. 'You have to be spontaneous sometimes, Callum. By the time I'd discussed it with you the thing would've been snapped up.'

'But your prized spontaneity has financial consequences,' Callum snarled. 'You know the budget for doing up this place; we worked it out together. Now, thanks to you we'll be servicing a credit card overdraft at some usurious rate of interest as well as trying to pay the bloody builders.'

'So what's your solution, take it back?' Sue shrieked in exasperation.

'No, of course not, we're stuck with this sofa now and we'll have to make the best of it,' he said, a shade more reasonably. 'But I warn you, Sue, I don't intend going to sleep on an argument either. That's never been the way things are between us. We don't hold grudges or sulk for days, we settle things then and there.'

'Fair enough, I'm not going to fight you on that point,' Sue said, mellowing slightly. 'We've got to resolve this row before the evening's out.' She walked over and placed her arms around his shoulders. 'I can think of one very good way of relieving the tension. A little horizontal jogging perhaps, test the springs on our newest piece of furniture?'

Her body pressed sensually against Callum, warm and curvaceous, perfumed and beguiling. It would be so easy just to segue over to the sofa and…

'Oh no, no, no.' Callum was determined. 'You are not getting out of your self-inflicted dilemma that easily, my girl. Beautiful as you are, it's going to take more than a fluttering of eyelashes and the promise of a conciliatory fuck to right this particular wrong. Were talking fifteen hundred pounds' worth of debt here.'

'So I've to suffer for my sins, have I?' Sue asked warily.

'Yes,' said Callum, once more in charge and with the look of a man with a mission, 'exactly that. A little bit of good old-fashioned punishment. After which,' he said, deliberately pausing to add *gravitas* to the statement, 'we are going to agree a series of penalties for any future misdoings which, knowing you, are more than likely to be evoked.'

Sue suddenly felt uneasy; disturbed by the rapid return of Callum's assertiveness she was thrown onto the defensive. 'Punishment? You can't mean, not physical punishment?'

'Oh, but I do,' Callum responded dangerously.

'But,' Sue was flustered, seeking a way out, 'I mean, I know in the past you've spanked me a few times before sex. It was fun, a little fantasy role play, indulging my submissive side by letting you play the master, but not real painful punishment.'

'If it doesn't hurt it doesn't work, Sue, and if you want us to finish rebuilding this house and keep living together you haven't got much alternative. None that I'm offering, anyway.' Callum was definite. 'We are about to begin a new regime which will, with any luck, curb your spending and reduce my blood pressure.'

'Keep us on speaking terms with the bank and save our relationship into the bargain, no doubt,' added Sue, with unwise sarcasm.

'I knew you'd see it my way,' he replied, ignoring the barbed comment, 'so we might as well start right now.'

'What?' she gasped. 'You can't, no way, I am not going to let you…'

'You don't have to let me, I'm going to thrash your pretty little backside whether you like it or not,' he snapped, sitting on the newly-purchased sofa and dragging Sue, kicking and struggling furiously, across his knee. 'And for a start we'll have this skirt out of the way and these knickers down.' So saying, he flipped the short flared skirt to Sue's waist and wrenched the offending panties to her knees.

'Nooo,' she wailed, a cold feeling in the pit of her stomach, aware this most certainly wasn't a game and that for once in her life she couldn't charm her way out. She struggled and kicked desperately, nevertheless, nearly catching him on the head with the heels of her leather boots, but ultimately no match for his greater strength and size.

Slap! Slap! Slap!

'I might be tight-arsed, but you'll shortly be sore-arsed!' Callum barked, struggling to hold the madly wriggling figure across his lap. If you're…' *Slap! Slap!* '…incapable of self-discipline…' *Slap! Slap!* '…you'll have to take the discipline I impose.'

'Owww! No, Callum let go, this has gone too far… oww, that hurts!'

Sue had adopted this position before, it was true, but that had been voluntary and humiliation was not on the agenda. Her cheeks had been no more than benignly warmed, Callum frequently stopping the spanking to pay pleasurable attention to her pouting sex. The mixture of ritual and a gentle, stinging sensation that soon suffused her skin and spread from her buttocks to her loins had been the ideal precursor to a prolonged and enjoyable coupling.

Not so now, each resounding slap across her naked nates stung and burned like the devil. Since it was

171

obvious his girlfriend was not going to take her penance meekly, Callum was forced to find other ways to prevent her escape. Choosing his moment he waited until her kicking feet had returned to floor level, and deftly swung his right calve across them, effectively pinning her legs and lower body to his knee. Sue's upper torso proved more difficult; her left arm was pinned against his hip, the hand largely preoccupied with maintaining balance, but the right continually sought to cover her bottom, spoiling his aim, so eventually he seized her wrist and forced it into the small of her back.

Sue moaned pitifully, aware her unwillingly proffered posterior was now fully exposed to Callum's punitive palm.

Slap! Slap! Slap!

Oblivious to her wails and pleas Callum concentrated on covering every last inch of Sue's lusciously rounded cheeks with ringing spanks, progressively turning the white skin a dusky red.

After five minutes, an eternity to Sue but seemingly half that time to her persecutor, Callum noted that her struggles had almost ceased. Exhausted by her earlier exertions, or simply resigned to her fate, Sue lay across his lap, whimpering softly. Callum stopped spanking, resting a hand on scarlet cheeks that were radiating heat like an electric fire. She moaned at even this soft touch, and a glance down revealed silent tears meandering down her face.

'I think I've made myself clear,' said Callum, unnecessarily.

'Yes, you brute,' came the sniffled reply.

'But before I let you up, I want to hear you accept that

any future reckless spending will be dealt with in the same way. Or rather,' he added after a significant pause, 'more severely.'

'More severely,' wailed Sue, as if such a concept were impossible.

'Correct. Overspend on furnishings again and you'll feel the hairbrush or my belt across that delinquent derriere. Now, do I have your agreement?' Callum reinforced the question with a final unrelenting blow across Sue's castigated cheeks, drawing a howl of anguish.

'Yes, I agree Callum! I'm sorry, really, please let me up.'

For the first time aware of a considerable distortion in his groin, Callum helped Sue rise stiffly to her feet, giving her tear-streaked, dishevelled form a conciliatory cuddle. 'All right, forgiven and forgotten,' he said. 'My, your bum looks hot and sore.' Sue mewed confirmation that it was. 'Kneel up on the sofa and I'll rub some cold cream on it.'

Which he did, tenderly and gently, Sue wincing and sighing all the while. As he carefully massaged the soothing balm into her ravaged moons, so she parted her thighs a fraction to reveal girlish secrets dewy with feminine damp. This unexpected development came as a surprise to Callum, and an even greater revelation to Sue. During her time squirming and suffering across his lap nothing was further from her mind than sex. Now, albeit still in some discomfort, a combination of his adeptly stroking fingers and the inexorable spread of heat from her tortured tush sent spasms of exquisite sensation to Sue's sensitive clitoris.

'Someone *is* getting aroused,' Callum observed.

'No, two people are already aroused,' said Sue, reaching behind to grasp the hardness distending his jeans.

'Better do something about it, then,' he suggested.

'You're not putting me on my back, not with my poor botty still feeling this sore,' came the smart rejoinder. 'Come and sit on the sofa where I can straddle you.'

'What about your knickers?' Callum croaked, quickly sliding into position.

'No time to take them off, I'm in a hurry,' gasped Sue, and despite being hobbled by the tightly stretched material she managed to move herself above him. Callum slipped two fingers inside her. Sue seized his impressive erection, and with tantalising slowness began to lower her soaking sex, groaning as inch by inch of him gradually filled her pulsating honeypot.

Urgently, breathlessly, the two began to fuck.

No gentle lovemaking, this, but a rapid rush towards the climax each so eagerly craved. Holding firmly to the back of the seat Sue ground down until their pubic hair entwined, leaning down to kiss him feverishly. Holding on to her waist Callum struggled to hold her in position as she bucked and writhed upon him.

Feeling his climax was imminent and sensing Sue was on the edge of hers, he relinquished his hold around her middle and cruelly gripped her scalding buttocks. With a shriek she came, slumping forward as a torrent of semen erupted deep in her vagina, and she lay physically and emotionally exhausted in Callum's arms.

Over the next few months Callum's system of fiscal penance was, just as he'd predicted, evoked on more than one occasion. As for its effectiveness, well, that's open to doubt…

'Oh, there you are, Sue. I've been reviewing our finances.'

'Really? I've been shopping, and found an amazing candelabra. Look, Callum, it'll make a brilliant table centre; just the thing to get the guests talking at the dinner party we've planned for your birthday… Why are you looking at me like that?'

'Because if our guests are talking about anything,' Callum glowered, 'it's more likely to be how we defaulted on the mortgage and got the house repossessed!'

'Oh, come on,' Sue lowered her gaze and pouted, 'we've talked about this before. It's no big deal; my man of the house here has developed the perfect system to sort out these little disagreements.'

'Don't go making big eyes at me, girl, and you can cut out the sarcasm too. My system was supposed to be an effective piece of behavioural conditioning. To wit, you associate spending money with having to sit on a cushion for the rest of the day. A simple equation; financial fecklessness equals a sore bottom.'

'And you did, too, you brute…' began Sue, in an unconvincing sulky tone.

'Once,' Callum interrupted angrily, 'before you used your,' he paused and gave a rueful smile, 'not inconsiderable sensual assets and feminine wiles to subvert the whole system, till what were meant to be proper punishments became just an appetiser for sex.'

'And you didn't enjoy it?'

'Yes, of course I enjoyed it,' he snapped, exasperated, 'as did you, which,' he went on suspiciously, 'no doubt accounts for your present state of attire.'

'Don't know what you mean,' she teased, flouncing across the room and bending low to retrieve a lipstick from her handbag. As she did so her short summer dress rose at the rear, revealing pert buttocks clad in alluringly brief white knickers. Sue maintain this provocative position while she repaired the ravages shopping had made to her lip gloss, then, with a coy look over her shoulder at the smouldering Callum, coquettishly wiggled her bum at him.

'Right, that's it, the last straw,' snarled Callum. 'You are really for it this time, young lady.' He grasped her by the arm and propelled her towards the sofa. 'I am going to put the *punish* back into punishment, earn a measure of respect from my delinquent wife, and,' he raised his eyes heavenward, 'put a stop to your ruinous shopping expeditions. The retail sector of the economy may collapse, the local stores will probably close, but at least we'll have a roof over our heads.'

He placed her, sitting unceremoniously on the arm of the sofa, which had begun these rows all those months ago. Her short skirt was now almost at crotch level, tightly around the tops of her thighs, toes hanging a few inches from the carpet.

'Sit on your hands,' he commanded sternly, and Sue, puzzled by the obvious failure of her usually infallible seduction ploys to provoke a libidinous change of heart, and not wishing to anger him further, obeyed.

With her palms effectively trapped beneath her buttocks she was in no position to defend herself from a sequence of stinging, utterly unexpected slaps to her bare thighs, which, unlike her bottom, were as yet unused to such robust treatment, quickly reddening under half a dozen ringing impacts from the perspex ruler Callum now held. 'Since basting your perfect little butt is obviously not having the required salutary effect, I shall clearly have to punish more sensitive parts,' he said determinedly, unleashing another salvo and drawing wails of protest in response.

Satisfied with the impact of his opening gambit he pressed home the element of surprise by pushing a shocked Sue backwards onto the sofa. As she toppled back he caught her up-swinging legs and held them above her head.

'Hands behind your knees and hold them up and back,' he growled, and Sue, anxious to avoid another unpleasant taster of the harsh ruler, obeyed.

Head and shoulders on the sofa seat cushions, hips raised by the padded arm, knees upon her chest, her rear end was now beautifully presented to Callum, who resumed his work with the ruler anyway. Thighs, the backs this time and every bit as sensitive as the front, calves and the broad cheeks of her bottom all suffered a series of smarting smacks.

'Ow – ow – ow – oh no, please, please Callum,' she protested, but to little avail. Only when a series of fine red lines marked her flesh from ankle to waist did he halt, a satisfied smile playing on his lips.

'Now I've got your attention…' he began, idly circling a finger around the gusset of her knickers, pulled tightly into her cleft and distinctly damp. 'Oh, what's this?' he continued, sliding an exploratory finger beneath the flimsy material to confirm his suspicions. 'We seem to be a little moist.'

'In which case, it's my body acting of its own accord,' moaned Sue. 'You needn't think I've any horny feeling towards you at the moment, you spiteful sod.'

'Maybe so, but you can't deny the physical evidence of your becoming hot and bothered,' he gloated, slyly feeding two fingers into the wetness of her sex.

'Time for me to take these knickers off you,' the deed rapidly followed the word, 'and for you to spread your legs wider.'

Shivering with involuntarily pleasure as his finger was pushed back between her labia, Sue followed his instructions and meekly parted her knees. Thoughts of chastisement yet again relegated to the back of his mind, Callum thoughtfully eased her discomfort with an adept finger-fucking, gradually drawing moans of delight from his subjugated partner. Then, with a succulent squelch, he withdrew his fingers, bent lower, grasped Sue firmly behind the knees and bought his mouth down to her sex. With practised ease he began to work his tongue up and down her glistening slit, rapidly flicking her clitoris, delicately circling the rim of her tightly puckered anus.

Scarcely able to hold her position, Sue wriggled and whimpered as waves of pleasure flowed through every part of her body. Urgently she pulled Callum round until he crouched over her head, whereupon she managed, using just one hand, to lower his zip and free the full length of his gloriously long cock. While he worked his oral magic on her, so she skilfully sucked and stroked his rigid erection.

Feeling events running ahead too rapidly, Callum reluctantly eased his throbbing prick from between her pouting lips, and looked around the room for inspiration.

Of course. As Sue lay, eyes closed in pre-orgasmic bliss, he tugged one of the candles from the expensive candelabra that had started this unprecedented sequence of events. Carefully, unhurriedly, he began to push its two-inch circumference into Sue's hot little haven. Bit by bit he turned and twisted the wax until only a fraction of its eight inches remained visible.

Sue lay incredulous, but glorying in the feeling of unbridled licentiousness. Holding her bottom cheeks firmly apart, Callum then took the candle's twin, and after basting the end carefully in her copiously seeping lubrication, pushed it against Sue's tightly tensed anus. 'That's it,' he encouraged breathlessly. 'Push against it, and then... good, in we go. Your cunt's completely filled with one thick candle – now I'm going to fuck your naughty little bottom with the other.'

Terrified less the fragile stick should snap, and amazed to find the ensuing sensations much more pleasurable than she could ever have imagined, Sue made no move to free herself. Once the second candle was inserted nearly as far as its companion, Callum stood back to survey his handiwork. His partner lay, undignified and undefended, open to whatever pleasure he chose, both orifices expertly filled with the birthday candles.

'Perhaps I should just light the wicks and see if the steady drip of hot wax onto your exposed flesh doesn't reinforce my no shopping message,' he suggested cruelly.

In response, Sue abandoned dignity, forfeited courage

and begged and pleaded as never before, promising him anything, anywhere, anyhow, but please to be spared such a torture. Callum made a show of relenting, though in truth he'd never seriously considered the proposition. Well, hardly.

Instead, he determined a compromise that entailed Sue having to await the conclusion of the ordeal. He left the room briefly without explanation, but it didn't take a genius to work out he'd soon return with some new implement with which to again castigate her poor sore buttocks, which turned out to be a series of soft leather thongs bound to a small polished wooden handle.

'As I said earlier, Sue, if simply punishing your bottom is not sufficient, I'll have to find other more sensitive areas, the better to convey my instructions. Which means, as you have discovered and as you are about to find out, your calves and your thighs.' His free hand delicately stroked them as he spoke. 'It also means,' he added, firmness and resolve once more in his tone, 'visiting other areas normally considered taboo by even dedicated CP enthusiasts, let alone occasional players such as ourselves.'

Sues eyes were wide saucers, her mouth gaping.

'Your breasts, vagina, the dark cleft between those peachy cheeks, every little bit of you will be visited to feel the full force of my disapproval. Every bit of your body will be dominated.

'You have no choice but to trust me not to go beyond your limits, but be warned, they'll be stretched like never before. In return, and in future, I'll be able to trust you to stick to our agreements. Won't I?'

'Yes,' she replied weakly, body tensed in apprehension.

Callum tucked her hands behind her head, enabling her to look down at her own sprawled form. Lazily he trailed the soft leather strands over her curves, dragging them over her breasts, brushing against each stiffening nipple, on across the taunt muscles of her stomach, circling the flesh of her parted inner thighs, watching her wince as the very tips brushed the dewed fuzz decorating her pubis.

Dextrously he flicked the very tips of the leather against her breasts. Sue watched in awe as the fair skin dimpled and swayed with each tentative impact, gradually harder, bringing more of each thong's length into chastening contact with the soft underswell of each breast, occasionally catching the erect nipples a glancing blow. Faint streaks of red appeared, each impact punctuated by gasps and squeals as Sue rolled her torso in response to the leather's caustic caress.

Callum worked methodically, criss-crossing her gym-toned abdomen, angling his wrists like a squash player to send little leather generated strands of fire slapping against her thighs, closer and closer until, '*Ah!*' the whip swung right between her legs and the strands slapped wetly against her sex lips, tightly gripping the girth of the candle. And more, each blow carefully controlled to push Sue further and further beyond the bounds of conformity and prior experience, until it seemed she could bare the tormenting sensations no longer.

Sue's moans grew louder, her hips jerking with each scorching strike; her inarticulate cries a mixture of distress and delight. Finally Callum could wait no longer, struggling to contain his erection, marvelling at both Sue's fortitude and her uninhibited response. It was high time to have his wicked way. Throwing aside the whip he bent and, with tantalising slowness, removed each candle in turn. Sue moaned with disappointment, feeling an empty void where moments before she'd been so pleasurably filled, pulsating with sexual energy.

'No,' she whimpered, 'don't take them away.'

'Oh yes,' he insisted. 'I decide what you get and when you get it, but don't worry, I'm not going to abandon you unfulfilled, not when you've been so brave.'

Lifting her limp form effortlessly he turned her face down over the sofa's accommodating arm, pushed her legs wide apart with his foot and grasped her hips purposefully.

'Yes…' she gasped dreamily, the cushion muting her plea. 'Oh, yes please, Callum. I've been *so* bad…'

Callum needed no second bidding.

So ready was Sue that his first thrust entered her to the hilt. Teasingly he withdrew until just the head of his prick separated her pouting lips, sliding it in just a little at a time.

'No, Callum, I need all of you. I want you deep inside me.' Sue's clutching fingers reached back, greedily searching for his hips to pull him forward.

He ploughed into her deep and vigorously, so deep and so vigorously that on each stroke Sue's toes were lifted from the floor, her tummy jerking on the padded arm as they rutted desperately against each other.

Callum fucked Sue through two successive orgasms, and somehow, with a superhuman effort, he managed to postpone his own climax. As Sue slumped on the cushions Callum carefully withdrew and squeezed his bulbous helmet, glistening with her copious juices, between her buttocks.

'Oh, Callum, I don't know if I can take it,' she mumbled. 'You've never fucked me there before.'

'You took the candle, and now you'll take my cock, and enjoy it, because I tell you to.' He placed one hand on her hip, the other on the small of her back. 'Up on your toes, girl, and push your bottom back. Good, now reach back and spread your buttocks.'

Meekly she obeyed everything, allowing Callum to relish the sight of his penis slowly stretching and entering her tight rear passage, inch by glorious inch until she lay impaled by his full length.

He slid a hand under her hips, eagerly sought her engorged clitoris, and began to stroke it while simultaneously sliding his cock in and out of her virgin rear.

This time they came together, finally laying exhausted, her sins atoned for. She had paid the price.

Stately Home

In a small room in a large mansion a girl waits in trepidation. Lit from a high window by the last of the sun's rays of the day, her predicament is witnessed only by the pictures on the walls. This is the butler's pantry, retreat and domain of that most senior of the servant class in the employ of Althorpe House, that most archetypal of English stately homes.

Bent forward, face down across a sturdy oak table the maid waits. Stretching to grasp the table's furthest edge she gazes straight ahead, nervously focussing on a framed black and white photograph hanging on the wall. The picture's subject stands foursquare and proud, wing collared, morning suited, inscrutable of expression, just as a good butler should be. For this is Forbes, the current incumbent of the pantry and the man responsible for the discipline of junior members of staff, which, when concerning as comely a figure as the one presented now, does not prove too irksome a task.

Legs perfectly straight, knees together, feet flat on the floor, stomach tucked in, bottom pushed out, like ticking off items on a shopping list the maid assumes the requisite punishment position without having to be told. High in spirits and, to her superiors if not betters, worryingly independent of mind, this girl has been here before; knows to lift her skirt to the small of her back, revealing trim, tautly-suspendered, black-stockinged legs. Knows not to lower her full-cut French knickers, for that is a task Forbes will attend to with unseemly relish, all the better to deliver a sound bare bottomed birching.

For that's what will follow this seemingly endless wait; no mere stinging hand spanking across his knee; no kneeling on a straight-backed chair to feel the razor strop's burning kiss. No, this unfortunate girl is to be birched, here below stairs, deep among the many corridors of this vast edifice of stone where she may protest and shout, kick and struggle, all to no avail as her alabaster-white skin is turned to pink, then red, and finally blazing crimson, with no one, save Forbes, to hear her cries. Be sure she'll eat standing and sleep face down for days to come, and all will know the price to be paid for disobedience, latitude and youthful *joie de vivre*.

Hark, she hears deliberate footsteps echo on the flagstones as Forbes walks purposefully down the hall. A smile flickers across his lips, a tear falls from the maid's eye. And after he's deemed her sufficiently beaten to purge her wrongs, real or invented, what then? Will she be taken by surprise, taken from behind with no choice but to lie there and think of England?

The year is nineteen-eighteen, but the scene could just as well be from any one of fifty years, before or since; it's happened before, and will happen again…

Janine sauntered over to the lofty bay windows and looked out at the Elysian expanse of carefully sculpted gardens stretching down to the languidly flowing river.

'A perfect setting, glorious unspoilt Kentish countryside, but just a short drive from the M25. Such well-preserved old houses are a rare find these days, and the garden's truly beautiful, albeit the planting's more than a touch eccentric in parts. Is it economically viable, though?'

Simon, standing by the fireplace, laughed easily. 'The gardens were dad's passion, and probably why the house has remained original; he never paid it much heed. No, the old man was always outside, experimenting with some new combination of species brought back from his botanical travels.

'As for the viability, well, that's your department, Ms Granger. You've seen the business plan. All I'm asking is a small start-up grant from the Heritage Commission. If our predictions prove correct Althorpe House should be financially self-sufficient very quickly.

'Two years ago I would have forgiven you some caution. But look at the facts: the economy's healthy, people have plenty of disposable income for trips out at weekends, and with all these gardening programmes on the TV interest in green-fingered activities has never been higher. Add to that the traditional British passion for gawping at stately homes, and I'd say our chances are good.'

Janine paced the room, deep in thought. A Liberty print dress swirled around shapely legs, her sensibly heeled sling-backs clicking on the Mendip stone floor.

Simon remained slouched against the hearth, prudently silent. At length Janine flicked backed her short fair hair and favoured him with an ice-melting smile; he was, she couldn't help but notice over the course of their several discussions, rather attractive.

'The problem is there are so many country houses open to the public these days, especially in the south east,' she said at last.

'London's still the biggest city and therefore the largest market,' countered Simon, his pronunciation of the last word noticeably hesitant.

'I know, horrid expression, isn't it?' said Janine. 'But that's how things are, I'm afraid. No more keeping beautiful properties for their own sake, it's all profit centres and bottom lines in the nineties, and I'm afraid your Althorpe brand... the name of the house,' she expanded in response to a further perplexed frown, 'isn't yet that well known outside the rarefied circles of architectural aficionados.'

Simon winced. 'On the plus side, and as long as it doesn't entail picking up a rake, the public love gardens and they're by far Althorpe's strongest point,' he countered again.

'No contest,' Janine raised her hands. 'Which is why, if you don't mind, I'd like just one more look around the house.'

This time Simon spared her the conducted tour and instead followed and lounged, insouciant, on pieces of worn but priceless antique furniture while Janine inspected each room. From time to time her gaze strayed from her assiduous note taking to peruse this handsome, laconic young man. Beneath the faded but expensive lawn-cotton shirt and battered cords she discerned the outline of a supple body, muscled by years of rugger and rowing.

His manner was characterised by the timeless charm and easy confidence that comes free with a public school and Oxbridge education. At first he'd seemed distant, but over the last few days Janine had discovered that beneath this initial reserve lay a mellow and mature charm, a welcome contrast to the pushy young accountants back at the office.

Not that Simon was the braying, chinless-wonder type, either. Far too smart for the guards he had, a brief résumé attached to the grant application told her, been something rather successful in the city until the unexpectedly early death of his father brought him back to the family seat in a last-ditch attempt to save it from death duties and a desolate future as time-share apartments.

'How many staff was there in the old days?' Janine asked.

'Up to twenty, with extra help hired from the village for special events such as garden parties and costume balls, during the house's halcyon period in Victorian times,' Simon told her. 'Even when I was young there was a cook, butler, two chambermaids – cleaners really, but mother preferred the old-fashioned title – and a gardener.

'Chambermaids, hm?' smiled Janine. 'Droit de seigneur, and all that.'

'No doubt about it, before the last war,' laughed Simon, unembarrassed and in no mood to repent the sins of his forbears. 'It's all very well to judge from the standpoint of today's values, but back then the social pecking-order was almost feudal, servants lived in, or at the very least in nearby cottages owned by the Althorpe estate. They didn't have the capacity to refuse his lordship, not if they wanted to keep a roof over their head.

'I'll plead innocence on behalf of my paterfamilias, though. Father only had eyes for mother, and his roses. But I wouldn't have put it past Forbes, our last butler, to try it on with the young lasses who worked here.'

'This must have been his domain, then,' Janine observed, as they reached a room at the foot of the back stairs.

'Yes, that's right, the butler's pantry,' Simon confirmed. '"Traditionally a room between the kitchen and larder for storing silver and china", or so it says in the draft text of the guidebook. Although, as you can see, Forbes made it into an exceedingly comfortable den. And why not? He did, after all, have complete power below stairs.'

'All the other servants had to obey him?' Janine asked, entranced.

'Oh yes, below stairs as above, it was a very hierarchical system. Answering only to the master, Forbes held sway. It's too long ago to recall clearly, but from what I recall of the school hols father pretty much abrogated all powers of staff discipline to him.'

'Which would account for this?' Janine asked as, heart pounding, she stooped to pick up a bundle of birch twigs from a bucket in one corner.

'Well, not those precise twigs. They were cut from the arboretum last week, as a matter of fact. But they're a pretty good update of some originals we found here.' Simon softly pushed the door shut as he spoke. 'There's something about the symbolism of that comparatively unremarkable little artefact that strikes a deep resonance with you, isn't there? I mean, despite the marvellous exterior details of this unique house, added to over four decades, something about the birch attracts you, doesn't it? I noticed as much on our earlier tour.'

Janine felt herself flush. There seemed little point in

denying the accuracy of the observation; he'd see right through any attempted bluff, better to try an edited version of a truth she wasn't yet fully comfortable with herself.

'Yes,' she said at length, meeting his forthright gaze as equally as she could. 'There is something about the power, the ceremony of its use that sends a shiver down my spine.'

'Not something you've ever encountered before, then? No personal experience, as it were?' Simon left the question open, and instead gently took the birch from her grasp.

'Not a birch, no,' Janine said slowly, evasively, acutely aware of the hot flush of incipient embarrassment starting to spread across her face.

'But something like it?' Some intuition told Simon he should push the point.

'Of similar purpose, yes,' Janine replied carefully, struggling to appear calm as her pulse raced madly.

'Ever thought you might like to sample the effect of its application?' Simon pressed, persuasively. 'As an experiment, perhaps?'

'Asking someone if they'd like to be birched seems to me the perfect example of an oxymoron,' retorted Janine, primly. 'And with someone I hardly know…?' She hesitated.

'But someone who can spot a kindred spirit when he sees one,' Simon continued with calm assurance. 'Who, to be truthful, deliberately left the birch there in the hope it might one day prove a catalyst to just such an encounter with a likeminded visitor. You've obviously done a thorough job in researching the business prospects of 'this stately pile, but what do you know of me, the owner?'

'Of you?' Janine was at once intrigued and puzzled.

'For example, that my now ex-wife – not blue blood, always headstrong – eloped with an Argentine polo player last March. But, in the three years we were together, knew exactly what she wanted, which was often a taste of the crop.' His voice had dropped to barely a whisper, soft but commanding. 'A wish I was pleased to indulge, after all, that was a large part of the attraction between us.'

'But…' Janine attempted.

'But what? I'm offering you the chance to indulge a very personal fantasy. No strings, no obligations.'

'But…'

Janine found herself uncharacteristically flustered, her prized professional cool rapidly deserting her. Rationally considered, her mind told her, this was clearly impossible, she should leave at once and pass the client on to a colleague.

And yet her heart spoke a contrary language, urging her on towards a quite different fulfilment. He was good-looking, the setting ideal, there'd never be a better chance.

'It's unprofessional?' Uncannily perceptive, he finished the sentence for her. 'You're entitled to a work break, and it's up to you how to spend off-duty time. No need to commit yourself immediately; consider the proposition overnight. You're due to visit tomorrow anyway with the decision on the grant. If you've still a mind to feel a birch across that splendid backside, be here at six. If not, we'll meet in the library. In the meantime, come here.'

Damn him. He'd seized the moment perfectly, acted

while her brain was still a whirl of confused thoughts and emotions. He'd not the slightest doubt she'd obey, and Janine swiftly proved his conviction well founded.

'All right,' transfixed, almost in a dream, she was belatedly aware it was she who had spoken.

'Excellent,' said Simon, enthusiastically. With no undue urgency he sat upon a sturdy dining chair and as she stood, uncertain, before him, she found herself incongruously puzzling whether it might be genuine Sheraton or a much later copy.

Reaching out to grasp her hands Simon pulled the novice female unprotesting across his lap. She let her body relax, the decision was made, the consequences out of her hands. Her gaze was initially directed at the carpet, now touched by the fingertips of one hand, and reaching up with the other she brushed hair from her face, tucking the strands behind her ear the better to look up and glimpse what the determined man had in store. She felt her nipples stiffen and a warm dampness between her legs.

Simon allowed himself a moment or three to relish the delightful sensation of her shapely form, warm and vibrant across his knees. Carefully he lifted the hem of her dress. 'This must, naturally, be on the bare,' he intoned softly, to himself rather than Janine, and before she could protest he slid her soft white panties to her knees, in a simple smooth movement.

Janine had evidently made the most of the summer thus far, her legs and bottom were perfectly suntanned, save for a pallid area a fraction wider than her cleft and pubis which roughly corresponded to the shape of an extremely immodest thong. Not as tanned though, thought Simon, amused at his pun, as they soon would be.

'Quite lovely,' he murmured, running his hands over her naked flanks. 'But then, I guessed they would be: long slender legs, flawless thighs, and a beautifully rounded bum. Perfection.'

Janine giggled nervously at the compliment.

'Be quiet,' he ordered, in a baritone voice of severity. 'This is no laughing matter, you're obviously long overdue for a thorough spanking, now get your head down, both hands on the floor, legs straight and push that bottom up.'

Simon began to slap the underside of each buttock, striking upwards with skimming strokes. The golden globes wobbled and danced beneath his palm, sending little shockwaves of delicious, tingling pain across her entire posterior. As her bottom warmed to his ministrations he smacked harder, concentrating on the spot where gluteal folds and upper legs meet, each jolt further stimulating her already engorged sex.

'I'm pleased to see you're making some attempt at modesty by keeping your legs together,' he said. 'Don't worry overmuch on my account, though... I'm sure the view will be marvellous,' he added, carefully spreading her thighs a fraction to afford a glimpse of soft, moisture-beaded pubic curls.

Emboldened, he began to spank more firmly, a dozen smacks alternating from cheek to cheek while all the time Janine became more excited as the stinging heat sent urgent messages to her pussy; perceptibly arching her back ever higher to each subsequent swat in a mute request for more. Hitherto largely silent, a series of sighs and whimpers began to escape her lips.

So this was what it was like to be on the receiving end of a man's hand, upended and vulnerable to a virtual stranger. She groaned; entranced by the sheer irresponsible wickedness of her behaviour she wriggled her rear in delicious invitation and sneaked furtive glances up at her tormentor.

Writhing on his lap, Janine ground her overheated pubis repeatedly against Simon's knee, determined to derive the maximum erotic pleasure from this most sensual situation. Her wetness and the distinctive aroma of feminine arousal was not lost on him, but he eschewed an immediate sexual response, instead sternly admonishing her to remain still and quiet, punctuating the command with slaps to her sensitive upper thighs. Wisely she took each subsequent volley without protest, meekly allowing her crimson orbs to be spanked further until she felt at least fifty applications of his punishing palm must have rippled and indented her painfully stimulated posterior.

All too soon he stopped and she was left gasping, her buttocks smarting and pink. Was that it? Was this as far as events would go? Her fantasies didn't stop here. The spanking was supposed to be just a preliminary. The young chambermaids summoned to this butler's pantry in times past had not simply been chastised, but their predicament exploited to the full. Taken roughly, like it or not, put to the cock good and hard and…

Frustrated and empty, Janine yearned for Simon to treat her thus. Oh, but she needed him, wanted to feel what, she fondly hoped, would be his substantial endowment slide inexorably into her sex and fill it to the brim. But instead, to her intense disappointment, Simon briskly restored her panties to their previous position and helped her, still shaking and unsteady, flustered and forlorn, to her feet.

'A timely reminder of what a proper spanking feels like,' he said, with infuriatingly self-possessed calm. 'But quite enough business for today, I think.' Efficiently he propelled her, bewildered and dumbfounded, though the door.

'I look forward to our meeting again tomorrow evening, should you decide to come. Until then, I'm sure you've plenty to think about. Goodbye.'

And that was it. Her executive status clearly counting for nothing, Janine, the proficient businesswoman – always to be relied upon to take charge of a situation – was politely but firmly dismissed from Althorpe House.

Part bemused, part angry and wholly frustrated, Janine pulled her convertible – roof down – into a shaded lay-by to the side of the winding drive and just short of the main gates. She could bear it no longer, so sliding her skirt up her bronzed thighs she tentatively slipped a hand into her damp panties. One, then two fingers eased shyly into her vagina, lubricated by the copious wetness of her unquenched desires. Pressing against her excited clitoris and with glistening fingers gliding in and out, Janine succumbed to a shattering, seriously satisfying orgasm, her head lolling back on the seat headrest, eyes shut dreamily, her breasts heaving slowly as she breathed deeply through slightly parted lips, the sun warming her flushed face.

Away in the distance, unobserved, a figure watched through a pair of binoculars from an upstairs window of

Althorpe House, and smiled…

The following evening Janine arrived five minutes early,
as was her habit with any appointment. Feeling strangely
at home and comfortable with the surroundings – more
so than with any of the succession of single-occupancy
flats she'd owned – she let herself in through a discrete
side-entrance and followed the familiar corridors to the
butler's pantry.

It was empty, so she waited, outwardly composed but
inwardly nervous and agitated. She looked around, tried
to imagine herself a servant in this room all those years
ago, considered the trepidation a young maid might feel
as she waited, straining to hear the approaching footsteps
of the butler. Once the stout oak door was shut no sound
from within these walls could be heard in the corridors
outside. And even if it could, who would take heed? Who
would take a chambermaid's word over that of the most
senior of all the servants? And what if he did thrash her
with more vigour and enthusiasm than some minor
misdemeanour might otherwise merit? And what if he
did afterwards, with her skirts still so immodestly raised,
have his wicked way? It was surely the prerogative of a
man of his experience and position and years of diligent
service.

The daydream served to calm her and, despite the first
faint stirrings of arousal, so her anxiety lessened.
Regaining her wits she examined the furnishings, and
discovered the birch in its customary place. She picked
up the awesome object, turning and flexing the pristine
shoots in her hands. Her bottom had felt the impact of
many an instrument of chastisement at the hands of

lovers. Initially puzzled, but ultimately lured by the prospect of the lubricious rewards this catalyst to her ardour might provide, several beaus had gladly indulged such wickedly submissive fantasies and played her favourite games. But none had taken the rituals as seriously as Janine, and the relationships had sadly not endured.

'I think you'll find it rather a superior example – extremely pliable.' Janine turned with a start. Simon had appeared soundlessly and surprised her, as had indeed been his intention. 'I see you've made your decision.'

He took the birch from her limp fingers, perused it closely and cut it several times through the air.

'Two decisions, in fact,' Janine replied, struggling to keep proceedings on an equal footing. 'Or don't you want to know the result of my report on the grant application?'

'Very much, but if I knew the outcome of your deliberations now it might prejudice what's to follow, and that,' he retorted calmly, allowing a short, dramatic pause to emphasise the importance of the words to follow, 'is just as important to me. Have you recovered from the spanking I gave you?'

Instinctively Janine's hands moved to stroke her buttocks, and she reddened at the memory of her acquiescence. 'C-completely, th-thank you,' she stuttered, thrown once more onto the defensive by Simon's sudden change of emphasis.

'I couldn't help but notice that from your point of view certain things were left somewhat, um... how can I put this politely... unresolved? That was almost an emergency stop you did at the end of the drive,' he added with mischievous guile.

This conversational *coup de grâce* caused Janine to abandon any further attempts to maintain her fragile poise. 'You *saw*?' she cried in a mortified tone, blushing furiously.

'Oh yes,' said Simon, unfazed and smiling broadly, 'most arousing. Made me realise I'd neglected my duties as a host. Please do accept my apologies.'

Damn him, thought Janine. Cool as a cucumber!

'I hope you've come appropriately dressed,' he continued. 'What say we do things properly this time?' The question was clearly rhetorical, since before Janine had the chance to reply he'd handed her two white scraps of cloth. 'Discard the jacket, pop these on, and you'll be the very model of a modern maidservant.'

Janine looked down at her clothes. She'd spent ages, and a great deal of care, getting ready. Never consciously intending to emulate the style of a servant, yet now, viewing her appearance objectively, it seemed so bloody obvious; her sub-conscious must have been working overtime. The plain white blouse and simple black skirt parodied uniform attire, so familiar a sight at Althorpe for more than a century. She wasn't even shocked by the modern lord of the manor handing her a white cap and apron, nor that she connived in the illusion by putting them on.

'Janine, you will do exactly as I instruct, any disobedience will earn you additional punishment,' Simon continued, as if her compliance was already a *fait accompli*. 'I'll happily repeat strokes or even begin from scratch. Now, move to the middle of the room, back straight, hands by your sides.'

Despite the fact that Janine had the power to ensure or

dent his financial future and he still blithely treated her like a naughty underling, she obeyed. She stood, erect and curvaceous in front of him, five foot six in black high heels, open-toed and fastened by a single strap. His gaze travelled upwards; firm, shapely legs, and above, he recalled with a pleasant shiver of pleasure, that superbly rounded bottom. To him the curve and swell of her buttocks were simply beautiful, and redolent of as yet undiscovered delights. Her attention-like posture thrust her breasts – the nipples clearly visible – against the silky fabric of her blouse. A faraway look glazed her hazel eyes, the weight of history hanging on her shoulders.

'You'll receive a dozen strokes,' Simon said shortly. 'And since I'm a kind master they'll be delivered in groups of four with a brief respite in between. Now to begin, touch your toes.'

Illuminated by a single shaft of evening sunlight from a high window, she bent gracefully from her narrow waist and grasped her ankles. Simon briefly set his hands on her hips, then, with tantalising slowness, he inched her skirt up her lovely thighs, past the dark welts of her stocking tops, followed the vertical line of black suspenders, and on over shimmering black knickers.

'Splendid,' he said approvingly. 'Stockings... they compliment your legs perfectly. Make sure you always wear them from now on.'

Janine waited, tensely aware of the golden rays spotlighting her predicament. She was embarrassed by his objectification, pleased by his compliments, and acutely conscious of the high heels thrusting her bottom into prominence. She grit her teeth and tensed her muscles, torn between wanting to get on with the ordeal yet dreading the first fierce stroke. Trepidation knotted her stomach, and arousal dampened her panties.

Simon took a step backwards, drew the birch to shoulder height and held it above his compliant victim. 'You may retain your knickers to begin with,' he told her. 'But stay in position or suffer the consequences. Ready?'

'Yes,' she replied clearly and firmly, bracing herself for the first stroke.

When it fell Janine at first felt very little; a swish of air followed by a rasping, prickly discomfort. Momentarily disappointment filled her consciousness, but then every inch of her buttocks abruptly felt as if the fires of hell had descended. It was all she could do to keep silent and maintain her balance, but the second stroke was already on its way. A blazing swathe of agony seemed to permeate her bottom. An involuntary cry escaped her lips. With hips writhing and hands struggling to maintain their grip she performed a staccato jig, much to the unseen amusement of her tormentor.

Oh, this was much worse than any beating she'd ever received before! There was no way she'd ever be able to take a dozen! No way her poor tortured bottom could endure even half that number!

Swit! The fourth stroke sliced down across the lower part of her vulnerable moons, abrading tender skin unprotected by even the thin fabric of her skimpy knickers. She gave involuntary voice to a cry that must have been audible down by the river. Her feet drummed on the floor, her lower body performed an involuntary twist routine, yet somehow she found the strength to keep her pose.

'Good girl, you've been trained well,' Simon said. 'Now stand up and put your hands on your head. No rubbing, that would lessen the beneficial effect.'

Her bum felt as if it had been branded and she longed to soothe the soreness away, but feared inevitable retribution if she did. She opened her mouth to speak, to explain she couldn't possibly continue, that this had been a leap too far, to plead if necessary – but no words came.

'I think we'd better find you something to hang on to for the next four, since you appear to find it so hard to keep still,' Simon continued. 'But first, be so good as to pull your knickers down.'

Janine felt her eyes dampen. The sod, she thought, struggling awkwardly under her skirt; he was determined to humiliate her. With as much dignity as possible she pulled the damp scrap of shimmering material down her thighs, and awaited his next instruction.

Simon turned her through ninety degrees, placed her face down over the sturdy table, feeling tremors course through her pulsating body as he did so. With practised ease he arranged her, legs straight, breasts flattened against the smooth, unyielding surface, head down, just so. He fussed around for several minutes, pushing her knees a little apart, making her wince with discomfort as he lightly ran his fingers across the red-flecked flesh of her stinging bottom.

The next four strokes came at regular thirty-second intervals. Janine clung desperately to the table's edge, the top cut uncomfortably into her thighs and felt cold against her naked abdomen.

Her sex, damp with arousal and visibly moist despite

her painful predicament, was clearly displayed to Simon as he methodically whipped her with the birch's cruel twigs. Please let him stop, she hoped fervently, but uttered no pleas for mercy.

However carefully cut, however skilfully rendered, the fact remains that following a few hearty strokes the twigs of a bound bundle of birch sticks twist and spread upon impact, projecting at odd angles and thus are likely to cruelly abrade areas beyond their intended target – and so it was with Janine. Errant parts of the punitive branch scratched and scored the soft flesh of her inner thighs, dug harshly and deep into her bottom cleft and, worst of all, castigated the soft labial lips of her protuberant pussy. But somehow, using reserves of endurance and fortitude she never knew she possessed, Janine maintained her submissive position.

She did now, however, give voice to her distress. Simon paused, let her regain her composure and then, with a firm hand, pressed between her shoulders. Janine writhed and twisted, moaned and cried, as the next two strokes brought her poor tortured buttocks to boiling point.

'*Please…*' she gasped after the eighth stroke, 'give me a minute.'

'Of course,' Simon complied, ever the gentleman. 'You've done well to stay put thus far, although such a beating would have been a good deal harsher in the old days.' Tears were meandering down Janine's cheeks and darkening the scrubbed tabletop. 'You look even more desirable dishabille,' he commented. 'To which further end I want those knickers right off for the final four.'

Janine groaned as she shimmied them over her shoes. 'Don't you think your naughty servant has suffered enough?'

'Do you?' he countered promptly. She nibbled her bottom lip in a way he found irresistible, frowned, and refused to reply. 'Well, I'm waiting?' he persisted, a warning note in his voice.

'No,' she said at last, voice barely louder than a whisper. 'I think I deserve to have my wicked bottom soundly whipped.'

'Then ask me nicely,' he said, standing close beside the table.

Wordlessly, Janine reached out and freed the hope of future generations from the confines of his trousers. Sheer pleasure quite literally engulfed him, and as her head bobbed rhythmically he leant over to caress her burning cheeks and slide a finger into her inviting pussy. Their breathing became increasingly laboured, their actions evermore frantic, and just when it seemed things would reach the point of no return Janine released him.

'Was that nicely enough?' she enquired seductively.

'Indeed,' he confirmed, forcing her again down across the table. 'Now, spread your legs wide and take your punishment.'

'Oh sir, must I truly be punished more? Surely a poor girl has suffered enough?' Janine's voice had changed in tone, the quiet Oxford diction transmuted to a more rustic sound. Either Janine was slipping ever deeper into her chosen role or, imperceptibly, there in the butler's pantry, some sort of temporal time warp had occurred.

'Indeed you shall, you insolent young trollop.' The words issued from Simon's mouth but were not of his choosing; instead he spoke as if some inward autocue had prompted them.

'Oh, but sir, the humiliation you heap upon me is beyond all reason, exposing my most delicate and private parts in such a way. Why sir, no one, not even my poor mother, rest her soul, has seen my sex and bumhole, laid open and vulnerable to be gazed upon in such a shameful manner.'

'Cease your complaining, girl,' Simon snapped, albeit in a voice which sounded eerily like that of Forbes, his father's butler and the last occupant of this since unchanged and atmospheric room. 'Over the next few months I intend to become a good deal more familiar with the downy crease that so insolently bisects this veritable peach of a bottom.

'You, young Miss Janine,' he continued, 'may count yourself lucky, for I like your bright, feisty spirit and quick mind, and have chosen you for preferment. From now on you'll work the upstairs chambers under my strict tutelage, and who knows, if you study hard and mark my instructions carefully, learn how to dress and act to please me, we may make something of a lady of you yet.'

'Oh, you tease me most unfairly, sir,' Janine whimpered. 'I cannot believe I should be selected for such a position.'

'Hush girl, over the months to come your application must be great, your discipline rigorous. If you are to better yourself then I must firmly correct even the slightest fault or deviation. I'll warrant before we're done your pretty arse shall taste the dubious delights of a razor strop and malacca cane cruelly wrought across the full and naked expanse of those fine young orbs.'

'Oh mercy, sir, you do so vex and distress me with

such threats.'

'Not threats, but a promise. And you say as no one else set eyes on such perfect private parts before, but your body betrays you even as you speak, young wench. See how your little cunt becomes inundated with libidinous juices at the very mention of chastisements yet to come. Why, already it is so well lubricated I'll warrant I can slide two fingers their full length within the honeyed portals of your vagina, just so.'

'Oh sir, no, I beg you, for no man has ever before penetrated my virgin pussy.'

'Do not pretend such modesty with me, you wet and wicked girl, for have I not seen with my own eyes your dallying in the hay barn with the young stable lad, his hand deep beneath your skirts? No girl, as part of your education you will learn to accept the lusty thrusts of a man, not the tentative fumblings of mere boys. I shall teach you to pleasure me as well as any adept and practised lover should, and in return I'll put all three of these tight little orifices to the cock and fill them to the brink.

'Now silence, enough dalliance and talk, brace yourself to endure the birch and mark my words, these strokes shall be the most severe you've taken yet.'

Janine felt sure her yells were audible half a mile away, but her chastiser remained unperturbed. Oblivious to her pleading, neatly side-stepping her flailing feet, he delivered four lusty strokes, patterning her buttocks and thighs with almost unbearable suffering.

Afterwards he allowed her to lie for several minutes quivering, sobbing, hands frenziedly massaging the punished flesh; unbroken but every inch a flaming angry scarlet – hot to the touch. Considerately he passed her a crisp white handkerchief to dry her eyes, and took a small pot of ointment from the mantelpiece.

'Traditional Victorian cold cream,' he explained, his normal voice restored, delicately rubbing the cream into her ravaged cheeks. 'We're hoping to sell it in the gift shop. Let's see if it's any good.'

Janine gasped and wriggled once again, but this time a good deal more pleasurably, as he skilfully soothed her blazing bottom. Fleetingly, deliberately, Simon's proficient fingers strayed, caressing her vulva, enticingly touching her sensitive clitoris, and pressing urgently upon her warm, inviting pubic mound. The insides of her thighs were wet with her juices. She heard the loosening of clothes, felt strong hands grasp her slender waist.

Greedily she pushed her hips back, impaling herself on his eager cock. He stood haughtily, letting her do the work, sensing her desperation to quell her need, then finally, just as Janine thought his teasing would drive her mad, he began to thrust… and thrust.

He fucked her, long and slow and deep. Sinking the full length of his cock into her welcoming sex, feeling her muscles tense to hold and squeeze his erection, creating almost unbearable sensations of pleasure for both of them. Infuriatingly, he'd withdraw until only the very tip nestled between her silken opening, then push forward again, shafting her to the womb.

Janine moaned, cried out, shouted his name, begged and pleaded for more of the same, harder and rougher too. She lifted her feet from the floor, clutched wildly at the table's edge for purchase, rolled her hips, demanded he grasp and squeeze her breasts, then finally, triumphantly, found her orgasm – and his too.

And, should you wonder, Simon got the grant money, and Althorpe House is now open to the public. Why not visit one weekend and soak up the atmosphere? Admire the gardens, and don't forget to visit the butler's panty – reckoned to be one of the most authentic and unspoilt. Perhaps treat yourself to a jar of locally produced cold cream from the gift shop; it's apparently very soothing.

You know, many feel the Althorpe House enterprise owes a large measure of its success to the skills of the professional business manager Simon had to appoint as a condition of the funding. Mind you, as an employee, Janine is subject to a strict disciplinary code, and aristocratic gentlemen are sometimes prone to take advantage of female staff; when they're allowed to, that is.

After all, as we begin a new century, traditional hierarchies are being subtlety eroded. There's even been talk of a management buy out.

Friday

Kay moved restlessly on the café's hard wooden chair. Invisible beneath her skirt a pleasantly warm sensation pervaded the flesh of her still tingling buttocks, but discomfort apart, she was glad to be sitting indoors; the walk from the car, a mere two hundred metres, had seemed – in her anxious state – to take forever. 'I often meet work colleagues here,' she whispered anxiously. 'What if someone sees me?'

'Smile and say hello,' he replied, unconcerned, enjoying her discomfort, both social and physical.

A group of youths looked in her direction as they traipsed in. She heard one comment crudely, and the others snigger. 'They're looking at me,' she whispered urgently, 'they're staring at my legs.'

'Quite probably,' he replied with infuriating calm.

Kay recalled his cool appraisal as she'd struggled to climb from the car with something approaching decorum. 'This skirt's too short,' she'd complained.

'Shorter than usual is all, and before you mention them again, your heels only seem high because you usually favour flats. You look extremely attractive, now do please relax.'

That was the longest sentence he'd spoken all morning and, she'd grudgingly admitted to herself, the analysis was largely true. Her skirt came perhaps four inches above the knee, and the shoes had three-inch heels.

Hardly a tarty ensemble, office workers in town routinely dressed in such a fashion, but her politically correct employment required a different orthodoxy.

So why was she dressed like this? Because he'd told her to. Why had she obeyed? Because she'd no choice. No, that was too naïve, too simplistic. There are always choices throughout our lives, albeit some more difficult than others. The struggles of the last century suffragists, feminism, were not for nothing. Kay could have stopped this peculiar relationship before it began, told this assertive man, the better part of a decade her senior, to do his worst. Let him report the results of his monitoring to her superiors, stand and fight her corner. She'd not done anything illegal, or acted for personal gain.

Just a few months before, had someone asked her what a firewall was, Kay would probably have guessed at some sort of safety precaution in the event of a conflagration in the office. Subsequently, patiently he'd explained to her it was no such thing. Not a physical entity at all, but a piece of computer software which allowed him to track and record details of the internet sites visited by every workstation in Kay's workplace. Installed at the behest of her employers, nervous at allowing workers too much freedom and anxious to stop recreational surfing in the firm's time.

It wasn't as if the web pages she'd visited were obscene or even pornographic. Just, well, Kay squirmed recalling how he'd accessed one of the addresses and confronted her with the half dozen grainy reproductions of young women on the receiving end of a soundly smacked bottom. Viewed, in the privacy of her office, on her PC, in company time.

She really had chanced upon the site the first time. After that the excuses ran out; she hadn't been forced to revisit it, or to find others, all with a similar theme. Of course if she'd known each hit was monitored, triggered by certain key words, she'd have been more discrete. But she didn't and since her computer at home was not yet connected to the internet it had seemed a harmless enough way to pass a tea break, her single-occupancy office door firmly closed against the world.

A little bit of excitement to brighten the day, something to look forward too with an enjoyable thrill of naughtiness. CP, as she'd learnt to call it, wasn't something Kay had ever experienced before, not as a childish punishment or lover's foreplay. Yet somehow those submissive poses fascinated and, not to put too fine a point on it, aroused her. Kay had begun to identify with the acquiescent woman in the pictures and stories, discovering that, far from cowed and battered, many had their own web pages within which they shared CP fantasies and sought the company of likeminded others. Which logically, Kay reasoned, meant she must be far from the only single woman viewing the sites and excited by their contents.

None of which helped her predicament one iota. For, as he calmly pointed out, such leisure pursuits were hardly what one would expect of a respectable charity fundraiser and not, he explained further, likely to go down too well with the avowedly feminist managers. However, he continued with disarming frankness, it so happened he shared her interest in such matters, albeit strictly from a dominant perspective.

He'd like to see more of her, and whether or not she

shared the sentiment there was now an orderly way to ensure he did so; his silence in return for Kay's compliance. And after all, if she visited such sites, wasn't such a liaison just what she wanted?

Kay had tried to explain her association with the subject was merely exploratory, untested, and theoretical. He was unmoved; the offer remained open but only for a limited period. Kay agonised for several more days before finally, reluctantly, acceding to his blatant blackmail, ambivalent about her decision right to the end. She enjoyed her job and believed it worthwhile. Career decision time; even if there was a matter of principal to fight, this one was unlikely to win her allies.

Fortunately he wasn't repulsive, which helped sway her judgement. Pleasant looking in a rather craggy outdoors way, clearly in good physical shape but, more importantly, a charming and amusing and above all intelligent companion. He had a propensity to always take charge, directing events with natural authority and an automatic assumption that she would do his bidding. He was confident, assertive, never rude or brutish, and too straightforward to ever be described as manipulative. True enough, Kay often found his instructions annoyingly constraining but, and here was the paradox, at other times she found his organisation of their time together strangely reassuring. What a relief to let someone else organise every detail for a change, to be absolved of all responsibility. After all, she thought, if she was coerced into something no one could criticise her for participating, could they? She wasn't to blame for the outcome.

Since when she had indeed been coerced into activities

the like of which six-month's ago she'd never have imagined. Kay smiled ruefully, a punishment that well and truly fitted the crime.

And, as time went on, she found the adult games he made her play increasingly arousing. She disliked the discomfort and pain, but revelled in the hot and heavy carnality that invariably followed, a complex juxtaposition of opposite emotions far beyond her previously pedestrian sexual encounters.

A touch of ego too, knowing this unusual man, who no more fitted the stereotype of computer expert than she did a closet fantasist, wanted her, desired her, took her. For the first time in many months Kay's life had a sense of purpose, she felt really alive. Far from surrendering control being a problem, his autocratic direction seemed to offer an almost perfect solution. Alone, she'd never have summoned the nerve to explore her fantasies, but now he made the sexual decisions.

Once or twice a month and always at his behest she made uninterrupted time for them to meet, a rare opportunity in most people's busy professional lives. Had she prioritised sex like this before, Kay thought, her marriage might have endured, instead of dissolving under the strain of two pressured careers. With subterfuge and ingenuity they synchronised diaries, created mythical appointments and told white lies. Just as some kidnapper's victims have come to empathise with their captors, so in Kay's case, gradually the bottom became complicit with the top.

Again she shifted uneasily on the seat. On the subject of bottoms, little did these precocious fellow customers know of the red stripes decorating hers, nor how they'd come to be there. Her concentration once again drifting from the present, she slowly reran the events of the last few hours through her mind…

Morning had broken, such a bright morning, and she'd enjoyed a leisurely shower while awaiting his arrival. She lingered in the bathroom, carefully applying the make-up he'd chosen, and dabbed on the perfume he liked. Appraising her reflection in the mirror, she felt the first lascivious stirrings start to disperse her apprehension.

In the bedroom she dressed carefully, following the E-mail instructions that had arrived on her PC overnight. Sipping a glass of sherry she slowly fastened the hooks of the waist-constricting black basque, and carefully straightened the sheer stockings of similar hue. God, what would her oh so respectable colleagues think of such a choice of lingerie. If only they knew, although of course the whole point of these liaisons was that they should not. Method actress-like in her preparations, Kay adopted a role along with the clothes. For a while at least she would leave the humdrum vanilla life behind.

As she did so she wondered what he would do with her – to her – on this occasion. The combination of anticipation and the memory of past encounters made her shiver with trepidation and good old-fashioned lust. This would be their sixth meeting, each more intense than the one before and, Kay reflected, there was never a more willing submissive.

She heard the key turn in the lock, the familiar footfalls as he crossed the hall. 'I'm here,' intoned a resolute, unruffled voice. Preparations completed, Kay walked downstairs to meet him. Dignified and composed, the silk gown loosely belted but failing to conceal her curves, she walked towards the fireplace in the lounge, gave a fashion model twirl and, just as his note had required, said simply, 'I await your pleasure.'

Wordlessly he sat on the sturdy sofa, watching her, enjoying the uncomplicated voyeuristic pleasure of perusing every inch of her body just as an artist appreciatively views the perfect landscape before picking up a brush. At last he reached out and pulled her to him, tipping her, unresisting, across his knee. No less than she expected; indeed, had he not done so disappointment would have far outweighed relief.

Calmly, methodically and exceedingly thoroughly, he spanked her. First over the thin tight fabric of her knickers and then, after taking an almost malicious delight in tugging the diaphanous fabric up over her cheeks and harshly into her bottom cleft, on her trembling bare skin which quickly turned a fetching rose-pink, causing her to utter the first audible reactions to her punisher's expertise. Breath quickening, a series of involuntary pants and cries escaped her lips, but drew no verbal response.

Interspersed with vigorous applications of his palm came interludes of respite, during which his hands delicately stroked and soothed the increasingly hot fullness of her buttocks, teased and explored the moistening crease between them. His left hand held her waist firmly as, ignoring what had now become cries of protest and childlike pleads for mercy, he continued the spanking, burnishing her backside from pale to red.

Squirming across his knee Kay knew better than to let

her hands interfere with his ministrations. Instead, she gripped the sofa cushions tightly, wriggling her hips and kicking her feet while her bottom burned and stung. After a while, in parallel with the soreness came another, more agreeable, sensation. A slow building feeling of unabashed carnality coursed through her loins and she craftily rubbed her moist-pantied mons against the muscles of his thighs to heighten her growing pleasure.

After the pattern of chastisement and caresses had been repeated half a dozen times he halted, and with a mixture of trepidation and anticipation Kay felt her knickers being drawn down to her knees.

Momentarily his hands rested on the two burning globes, hitherto concealed by the scrap of cloth. She lay meekly, unsure what was to follow, as he prised apart her thighs, his fingers gently spreading her labia to reveal the promise within. Kay yelped with shock as something hard, smooth and spherical was insinuated between her engorged nether lips and deep into her vagina. Another similar push and a second such object joined it.

'Japanese love balls,' he explained dryly. 'The more you wriggle the more they'll stimulate you from inside.'

The next ten minutes passed in a blur. As Kay's arousal increased so her capacity to endure ever harder slaps rose. Squirming in response to each successive slap set the two balls in motion within her, making waves of pleasure pulse through her aching clitoris.

'Sit up,' he said suddenly.

'Why?' Kay whispered instinctively, and instantly regretted the perceived insolence of her question as her thighs were peppered with a volley of stinging slaps.

'You don't learn very quickly,' he said, lifting Kay

215

into a sitting position on his knee. Humiliated and undignified she prudently sat silent, gown around her waist, knickers around her knees. He laughed, delighted at her confusion, and then without ceremony tipped her back onto the sofa, holding her ankles aloft with one hand and exploring her hot little sex with the other.

Kay's face blushed as red as her lower cheeks. Fully exposed she was powerless to protest as he tugged at the cord linking the two love balls, sending electric jolts of excitement coursing through her. Laconically he manipulated her clitoris with his thumb while at the same time a nimble finger teased her tightly puckered anus. Meanwhile a harder hand soundly spanked the expanse of her buttocks. Kay's nylon clad legs kicked in anguish as the last areas of smooth white skin were mercilessly attended to. Her gabbled words became a mixture of petulance and pleading. Friends and colleagues at work, her former husband, none could ever have believed she would so crudely and urgently demand to be fucked.

'When I'm ready,' he replied, unflustered, still neatly attired in sharp contrast to Kay's dishevelment, 'and not before. What you want and I allow are two very different things.'

Roughly he heaved Kay unsteadily to her feet, pulled the tangled wrap from her and rotated her by the shoulders to gaze approvingly at the glowing crimson orbs of her behind.

Turning her again he pushed her backwards. Handicapped by the high heels she thought she would fall, but was thankfully halted by the padded back of an easy chair, companion to the sofa, against which she now leant, facing him, her hands trapped behind her. Grasping her hair he kissed her long and hard, Kay responding vigorously, pushing her tongue deep into his mouth, grinding her body urgently against him. Without preamble or finesse he tugged down the top of the basque to reveal pink nipples, erect and available. Using just his finger and thumb he roughly twisted and tormented each hard protuberance, making her gasp and groan.

Next, in the manner of a magician, he produced an old wooden school ruler, apparently from nowhere. Instinctively she shrank back, but to no avail. Carefully, deliberately he slapped the underside of her exposed breasts, clearly enjoying the spectacle of them quivering before him with each cruel impact. Hands pinned beneath her, unable to protect herself, Kay could only yell loudly in protest. Meanwhile her sex glistened wetly, her traitorous libido again betraying her.

Apparently satisfied with the angry red blotches he'd visited upon her breasts, he turned his attentions to the front and insides of her tender thighs, no longer concerned to allow Kay even the lightest of soothing touches, but instead cruelly indulging his dominance.

Stoically enduring this latest onslaught, Kay sensed a conclusion was not far off, saw the growing bulge in his trousers, heard his laboured breathing, recognised the obsessive glint in his eyes.

Holding the ruler vertically he challenged the last taboo and directly, softly, spanked her wet sex lips. Struggling vigorously in response, she finally freed her hands and tore at his belt, attempting to free his erection. But to no avail, on this occasion the final penetrative pleasure was to be denied. Instead he ground the heel of his hand hard against her overheated sex. A diabolical combination of the love balls within her and fingers teasing her clitoris proved too much. Kay climaxed but, just as he'd intended, remained unfilled.

Permitting her no time to repair her appearance he abruptly handed over her clothes and lipstick. 'Get dressed, we're going to lunch now,' he instructed, and knowing it was useless to protest, she obeyed.

Within minutes Kay was sitting meekly in his car, with no idea of their destination. Desperately frustrated, she wondered what more she must endure that day…

'Kay.' Shaking her head and struggling to focus on the present she returned to reality: the café, the conclusion of their lunch.

'Sorry,' she replied automatically.

'I said,' he repeated in a chilling tone, 'this afternoon we're going for a walk in the woods.' Then, lowering his voice still further, added, 'You won't be requiring your knickers, so be good enough to hand them to me.'

Kay blushed vividly, but eager not to antagonise him by being tardy in response, she pushed back her chair. 'I'll go to the ladies and take them off now.'

His gaze was unwavering. 'That won't be necessary, you'll take them off here.'

'Here?' Kay's incredulity sent her voice up an octave, the pitch attracting glances from at least two other tables. 'Here?' she repeated in more measured tones, trying to reconcile inward pangs of anxiety with the sensual signals transmitting through her nervous system. 'I can't…'

'You'd better,' he replied coolly, 'unless you relish being spanked for your disobedience, in public.'

It took a few minutes of furtive, embarrassed fumbling,

twisting and turning – during the course of which a passing waiter was treated to a salacious glimpse of stocking tops and a little beyond – before a mortified Kay was able to inch the black lacy scrap over her ankles and pass it to him, who'd sat smiling enigmatically throughout the entire performance. 'Thank you,' he said, 'I'll settle the bill and we can begin our stroll.'

Although relieved to be out of the café – she was convinced some of the diners were aware what was going on – Kay was too worried at what he had planned for her to enjoy her temporary respite from torment.

Fortunately the woods formed part of a local park, apparently deserted save for a solitary dog-walker several hundred metres away.

Kay winced as he squeezed each bare buttock through the thin material of her skirt. 'Ow, don't you think my poor bottom's suffered enough?' she complained.

'I take it that was a rhetorical question,' he replied, grasping her elbow and steering her from the late summer sunlight-bathed path to a less well-used gravel track, darker beneath the spreading overhang of trees.

'The council has planted quite a variety of young green leaf samplings in this section,' he said conversationally. 'Just the thing for my little experiment.'

Stopping, he reached up to examine a thin, supple, gently curved branch. 'Hmm, a definite possibility,' he said, reaching into his pocket for a penknife and cutting a length about a metre long.

A look of concern crossed Kay's face, 'Experiment, with that?'

'Exactly,' he said, pleased at her acuity. Deftly he stripped off the leaves to leave a pliant switch, which he flicked though the air with evident enthusiasm. 'This, if I'm correct, is an ash. A little further on we should at the very least find hazel and birch.'

Kay shivered as the whippy wand whistled through the air.

'The experiment being, which is the better to thrash you with,' he added helpfully.

'So, we cut a bundle, take them home and I get beaten with all of them?' Kay guessed.

'Not exactly,' he smiled. 'I rather thought we'd try each in situ – alfresco, as it were, then take the best one home.'

'Whip me here, in a public place? People might—'

'Yes, very true, adds to the spice, doesn't it?' he interrupted eagerly. 'Now, bend over and touch your toes, my dear.'

Kay looked around frantically. Fortunately not a soul was in sight, but the more she prevaricated the greater the chance of a passer-by chancing upon them. So she bent and clasped her ankles, then gasped as her skirt was lifted onto the small of her back. 'Oh no—!' but her protest at the unexpected baring of her bottom ended abruptly as the first searing cut bisected the still rosy cheeks. A line of pain quite unlike either the cane or crop, both of which she was now intimately acquainted with, took her voice away. She rocked, squeezed her ankles for support, and another equally agonising stroke landed a centimetre or two below the first.

'Yeow!' she wailed.

'Shh, have some consideration,' he chided, 'people come to the park for piece and quiet. Still, I see what you mean, that certainly does leave a mark. I think a brace will suffice for now. Follow me.'

He strode ahead, leaving Kay to struggle upright and stagger stiffly after him, rubbing her seared seat through the now chafing material of her skirt.

The hazel was, if anything, worse. Bent at the waist and clutching her ankles for the second time, two more strokes etched into her overheated moons, Kay had tears in her eyes as she tried her most pleading expression on her tormentor. But us usual pleading, mutely or otherwise, had zero benefit.

'Just the birch to come,' he said.

Fortunately he was skilful enough not to overlap the final two strokes onto earlier wheals. Had he done so Kay might not have caught a glimpse of movement or managed to stifle her cry into a cough and lurch upright as an elderly woman walking what appeared to be a rat on stilts rounded the corner.

'Morning,' he hailed, briskly striding on, the flexible little branch still in his hand.

'Morning?' replied the women, looking at her watch to confirm it was early afternoon, before fixing Kay with a long enquiring look as she passed.

'Slow down,' begged Kay, 'even walking is sore.'

'Yes, perhaps a tad more severe than I'd expected,' he said, without hint of apology or accountability on his part. 'The question is, which to choose? Any preference?

'We'd better save the old birch for another time,' he answered his own question upon receiving nothing but a sulky silence. 'It spreads its favours a little widely, I feel – or more correctly, you feel. Likewise the hazel. Therefore, I think we'll stick with the ash; better accuracy, more control.'

Decision made, they walked back to the car in contemplative silence.

For their next meeting Kay was summoned to join him for a long drive, during which he indicated he had important information to impart.

'So far,' he explained, 'you have done very well, pleased me greatly and adopted the role of submissive better than I would have hoped. And you have learned important lessons about yourself in the process. I've punished you in private and increasingly forced you to act out aspects of your role in the public domain. Heightening the risk of embarrassment or, worse still, recognition, yet simultaneously enriching each scenario and its subsequent sexual conclusion.'

'Will there inevitably be a sexual conclusion?' Kay asked hopefully.

'Oh yes.' He was unequivocal. 'Discipline has definitely improved your demeanour, but must also prepare you to explore the further limits of sex. I seek not to make you passive but to ensure an erotic response that will provide pleasure for both of us. You may not,' he smiled, 'always enjoy the journey, but you should derive pleasure at its end. If not I have failed in my self-appointed role and must release you.'

'You have changed my sexuality irrevocably, it's true,' she agreed. 'I'm often scared, usually made to suffer, but rarely unsatisfied at the close of an encounter. I would not have gained such knowledge of my own carnal needs had we not met.'

'And more to come,' he said. 'I warn you, Kay, soon I intend to take you further and test your obedience to the limit. Our situation has become too cosy – we must test the boundaries.'

And with that declaration, he infuriated Kay by driving her straight home, declined her invitation to go in, pecked her vaguely on the cheek by way of parting and drove off.

Her feeling of desolation lasted for days, but whether it was him or what they got up to together she missed, she honestly didn't know.

Mindful of his threat to 'test the boundaries', Kay waited for his next summons. The following days were spent on an emotional edge, half hoping and half dreading he'd call.

Fortunately, when the call came, she had no plans for that weekend, but knew in her heart she'd have ruthlessly dropped family and friends in an instant to obey him. Not once did it ever occur to her to question, negotiate, or simply ignore even the most irksome of the duties he had blithely commended her to undertake.

Smiling brightly and completely at odds with those aspects of his character he so far had chosen to reveal, the man in question arrived promptly outside Kay's flat at eleven on a fortunately sunny and rain-free Saturday morning.

Nodding approvingly as she walked out to the car in the prescribed apparel, he made no effort to help with the heavy leather holdall she carried. 'Just toss it on the back seat and hop in,' he said by way of welcome, yet despite the casual tone the mere sound of his voice was sufficient to send a shiver of pleasure up Kay's spine.

Previous experience had led her to practice the art of entering a low car decorously, but as she swung her legs

223

next to his the belted raincoat parted about her thighs to divulge her quiescence in wearing very little underneath. Momentarily visible to anyone with snapshot vision, were sheer honey-toned stockings fasted to black suspenders, and a carefully depilated bush. But what couldn't be seen was a fine silver chain that circled her waist, and her breasts unfettered, the nipples deliciously stroked by a black silk chemise.

Another silver chain hung around her neck, and matching slender rings adorned the index finger of each hand and pierced her ears.

'You're looking lovely,' he said simply, and Kay beamed at the recognition of her efforts. In response he laid a proprietorial hand on her thigh before, somewhat to her regret, moving it to shift the car into gear.

After only half an hour he braked at the last moment and swung the roadster into a short drive, a quick burst of acceleration along a tree shaded track and the vehicle crunched to a halt on the gravel in front of a large country house.

Vaulting out of the driver's seat without recourse to the door he strode around to the passenger side and helped Kay out. 'Go on in,' he said, gesturing towards the front door,' and followed her inside.

He unlocked a stout oak door in the far corner of the hall and Kay found herself descending a spiral staircase of cast iron, and she realised she was in what had once been the cellar – now transformed into a dungeon!

Carefully locking the door behind them her joined her at the foot of the steps. Speechless, Kay could only stare around her, whether bemused or amused even she didn't know.

'I managed to get the use of the place until tomorrow evening,' he stated, answering her unspoken question. 'We're totally self-contained, and as you can see, fully equipped.'

Which, Kay could see, was something of an understatement.

There were ceiling and floor rings for securing hands and feet, a stout wooden whipping post, and a vaulting horse with ankle and wrist restraints fitted to the legs. There was a bed, similarly equipped with tie-down points, and there was a good stock of footstools, bolsters, even the traditional straight-backed chair to provide any position one might desire. The oak table looked extremely sturdy, but the wardrobe had a more passive purpose; he opened the door to reveal rows of neatly folded and hung costumes.

'All the obvious clichés, I'm afraid: maid, nurse, parking warden, airhostess… along with some rather nice historical stuff: Regency, Victorian, and some rather brief modern affairs in leather, rubber and PVC.

Clearly at ease with his subject, he opened a large blanket chest and beckoned for Kay to look inside. Her blood raced at the sight.

Carefully arranged in drawers was an arsenal of instruments of correction: Tawses and straps, crops and martinets, whips and paddles. At least a dozen canes of varying size and thickness, and one section seemingly devoted to pressing household items into a service for which they were never intended; hairbrush, plastic spoon, wooden spatula, a bundle of birch twigs, belts, a razor strop and others barely glimpsed.

'You're not saying much,' he prompted, 'or indeed,

anything.'

'I,' Kay croaked, her throat suddenly dry. 'I don't know what to say. You warned me to prepare for something special, but this—'

'I intend only for you to sample the merchandise,' he cut in. 'Not tie you to each and every piece of apparatus, nor flog you with every implement in the room. Locking the door was merely a precaution to protect the outside world from us, not to hold you captive. You are free to leave at any time, but within this domain you defer to me always.'

He pulled her to him, looking at her closely with compassionate but steely-blue eyes.

'Our relationship has reached a plateau; we can continue, or we can part. If we are to go on we must be sure, of each other and of what we desire. If you commit to me I promise monogamy, fidelity and security. A degree of independence in matters professional and official, but when we are together I shall be in control; your submission given freely but once proffered, complete and utter.

'Make no decision now, let events take their course and in the morning I shall respect whatever destiny you choose.'

Up until this moment Kay's heart had been beating furiously, fuelled by a heady mixture of excitement and anxiety. Unaccountably this bewildering collation of emotions was replaced by a feeling of calm certainty. There was no need to debate her decision for the following few hours, they need live only for the moment.

'I choose to stay and play,' she said plainly.

'Wonderful.' His pleasure at her words was

transparently obvious. 'In which case you can expect to be thoroughly dealt with.' Stepping behind her he slid the raincoat from Kay's shoulders, leaving her with little modesty, nor even a scrap of material to shield her bottom and most private parts from his lascivious view. He led her forward to the centre of the floor, where two loops of soft rope hung from sturdy hooks in the ceiling.

'Reach up,' he commanded, binding each wrist until she was stretched, allowing the rope to take just a little of her weight, arms out flung like a supplicant, bound and helpless.

Kneeling, he paused to savour the sight of her freshly shaven labia. Sliding a hand up each shimmering stockinged leg he nudged both her feet outwards until the apex of her thighs, down to the teetering heels, formed an inverted V, then bound her ankles with two more soft strands of rope to large rings set into the floor. For the first time since they had met, Kay was totally enslaved.

'Henceforth you don't move without permission,' he said shortly. There was clearly no possibility of argument and Kay, aware it was no longer her place to talk, said nothing.

She shivered with an adrenaline rush of delight at the feel of his touch, as he delicately lifted the chemise to bare her breasts. Deft fingers gently twisted her nipples, which swiftly stiffened in response. Palms cupped each soft globe, and his chest pressed into her back. Kay swayed, arching her body, pushing her bare buttocks back against the firm erection she could already feel through his trousers. As if from the perspective of a spectator, she heard herself utter a deep groan of pure animal lust.

And then her tormentor was gone, leaving her hanging

alone. She needed more, much more. She longed for his touch, to feel his possessive hands on her.

'Bad girl,' said a stern voice, close by. 'Bad girl. Have you any idea what a lewd exhibition you're making of yourself?' As he spoke he swept back her hair and blindfolded her with a long black length of silk. All too briefly his lips brushed her earlobe, and then she stiffened and yelped in shock as a vicious hand slapped her bared buttocks without warning. Her poor bottom throbbed, but gradually the sensation became somehow pleasant, transforming into glowing warmth.

Scarcely had she recovered, when she sensed rather than felt him kneel before her. Her sex pulsed with expectation, and this time she was not disappointed. Roughly he grasped her hips and lightly ran his tongue over her pubic mound, the hairless skin gleaming with feminine juices. Minutes passed blissfully and she emitted groans of delight, grinding her hips forward to relish every probing touch of his skilful tongue; circling her engorged clitoris, pushing rudely between her labia, gently teasing the soft folds, laving them with his mouth and gently nipping her inner lips between teasing teeth.

Kay panted, moaned, implored, careless of the spectacle she presented, dignity long sacrificed to the goal of achieving a shattering climax, no matter what the price. Then, again he was gone, leaving her aching and empty once more, a confused mixture of frustration and craving.

'You weren't given permission to move,' admonished a noticeably colder voice.

'How could I not, with you tonguing me?' Her words seemed to hang in the air, affording her ample time to regret them. She heard him move away, a faint rustling sound, then an even slower return followed by another long silence, during which every muscle of her body tightened. She waited, tense with apprehension, suffused by a heady mix of fear and expectation.

Still the first stroke caught her unawares, but she recognised the crop immediately; by sound as the leather flaps slapped into her right buttock, by feel as the sharp linear sting made its blazing presence felt. Three more perfectly horizontal strokes landed, each delivered with a deceptively strong flick of the wrist, her pale flesh quivering at each sharp impact.

Mercifully he then halted, enabling Kay to catch her breath while a deep, burning smart spread through her defenceless, involuntarily twitching orbs. Then again he caught her unawares. This time the very tip of the crop flicked the underside of her swollen breasts, catching the erect nipples, marking her beautiful breasts with angry red blotches. She cried out in hurt and consternation, twisting on the rope in a fruitless effort to escape.

Another wait, another silence, darkness, breasts and buttocks throbbing madly, each punished pair craving soothing caresses that never arrived. But now she understood. Was not even startled when the chastising crop revisited her hindquarters, harder this time – real scorchers. Damn, she thought, but he was certainly laying it on, employing the full springy length of the instrument's shaft to make her firm mounds glow hot and sore.

The pattern continued, a pause, then four strokes to the upper fronts of her legs, leaving stripes visible through the darker welts of her stocking tops, the crop's extremities aimed with wicked accuracy to lash her tender inner thighs.

Another pause, then four more cuts lashing the backs of her thighs, no painful pleasure now, just plain stinging agony, bringing a complaint to her lips and tears to her eyes.

Time ceased to have meaning. He could, perhaps even would, continue indefinitely. Kay had no protection other than an abiding trust in his awareness of her limits.

Yet another pause, then the assault on her buttocks again, this time the blows crossing previous sore stripes, causing crossroads of intense discomfort, making her hips jerk and weave in a frantic dance of despair.

'Oh no, *please*,' she shrieked, regardless of self-respect, glistening tears squeezing from beneath the blindfold as she begged for clemency, heels tap-dancing a mute protest as her body endured a mass of diametrically opposite sensations. The heat from her soundly beaten bottom spread between her legs, her sex already wet, fuelled by her desire and his skill.

He let her wait, sightless and suspended, unsure where and when, if at all, he might strike next. She could hear his breathing, now almost as heavy as her own, sensed his need, proof that even he was subject to the same forces of arousal and desire, shared her urgency, ached for closure. She wanted him deep inside her immediately; but nothing he could do would make her speak the words out loud. He was the master, therefore he must decide.

Which he did. Deft fingers freed her ankles, untied her wrist, forced her to squat in front of him, held her hair, freed his cock and fed it between her lips, urging her with crude words to suck, to run her tongue along the full length, to bring his erection to its full potential, the better to fuck her with.

Kay's jaws were beginning to ache when he tugged her abruptly upright, pushing her across the room to kneel head down, buttocks raised, knees spread, on the bed. Six more cuts of the crop bit across the rear she so brazenly presented for his pleasure. Delivered vertically they sliced across the earlier weals, leaving marks that would be visible for days. Taking advantage of her aroused state to up the odds, he scorched the crop into her buttock cleft, the crop's tip flicking cruelly against her tightly puckered anus.

Consumed by a wave of lust Kay pushed out her punished posterior, her labia pouting in invitation, craving satisfaction and release. Her chosen master entered her without subtlety, holding her hips and sinking his full length deep inside her, fucking her urgently.

Kay orgasmed almost at once but he, always the one in control, somehow managed to hold on, dragged a couple of pillows beneath her twisting hips and pushed her forward to lay flat upon the bed. Dazed by the sheer force and intensity of the experience she could only writhe and mew softly as she felt a probing finger smear cream, cold and slippery, around her anus, searching out the small opening, plundering her final secret.

Slowly, tenderly, he fed his full length up inside her and with short careful strokes began to fuck her arse. The forbidden pleasure of doing something so taboo was enough to catalyse Kay's second coming, and this time they reached their climax simultaneously.

Two days later they lunched in their favourite café again, Kay flushed and dreamy, sitting with care; her haunches still inflamed with the aftermath of his punishment, her vagina and anus pleasurably pulsing, evidence of their passion.

'What are you thinking about?' he enquired.

'Our weekend of basic naughtiness,' she replied. 'I suppose it's back to reality now,' she added, regretfully.

'We can create our own reality,' he told her, 'if that's what you decide.'

'I've experienced, I've thought, and I've reached a conclusion,' she stated. 'Let the ritual of pleasure and pain endure. Continue to change my life, if you will. I want you as my master.'

More exciting titles available from Chimera

* * *

All **Chimera** titles are available from your local bookshop or newsagent, or direct from our mail order department. Please send your order with a cheque or postal order (made payable to *Chimera Publishing Ltd*) to: **Chimera Publishing Ltd., Readers' Services, PO Box 152, Waterlooville, Hants, PO8 9FS**. Or call our **24 hour telephone/fax credit card hotline: +44 (0)23 92 783037** (Visa, Mastercard, Switch, JCB and Solo only).

To order, send: Title, author, ISBN number and price for each book ordered, your full name and address, cheque or postal order for the total amount, and include the following for postage and packing:

UK and BFPO: £1.00 for the first book, and 50p for each additional book to a maximum of £3.50.

Overseas and Eire: £2.00 for the first book, £1.00 for the second and 50p for each additional book.

*Titles £5.99. All others £4.99

For a copy of our free catalogue please write to:

Chimera Publishing Ltd
Readers' Services
PO Box 152
Waterlooville
Hants
PO8 9FS

or email us at:
sales@chimerabooks.co.uk

or purchase from our range of superb titles at:
www.chimerabooks.co.uk

Sales and Distribution in the USA and Canada:

LPC Group
1436 West Randolph Street
Chicago
IL 60607
(800) 626-4330

* * *